Charles Thomas Samuel Birch-Reynardson

'Down the Road'

Or, Reminiscences of a Gentleman Coachman

Charles Thomas Samuel Birch-Reynardson

'Down the Road'
Or, Reminiscences of a Gentleman Coachman

ISBN/EAN: 9783744734981

Printed in Europe, USA, Canada, Australia, Japan

Cover: Foto ©Andreas Hilbeck / pixelio.de

More available books at **www.hansebooks.com**

REMINISCENCES

OF

A GENTLEMAN COACHMAN.

LONDON : PRINTED BY
SPOTTISWOODE AND CO., NEW-STREET SQUARE
AND PARLIAMENT STREET

CARRIAGE OF A DOVER ROAD

THE MAIL — 'the celebrities on the heads of 30 shire hill, Dover.'

DOWN THE ROAD

OR

REMINISCENCES OF A GENTLEMAN COACHMAN

BY

C.T.S.B.R.

BARBITON HIC PARIES HABEBIT

LONDON: LONGMANS, GREEN AND Cº.

OR

REMINISCENCES

OF

A GENTLEMAN COACHMAN.

BY

C. T. S. BIRCH REYNARDSON.

-

SECOND EDITION.

LONDON:

LONGMANS, GREEN, AND CO.

1875.

TO THE

RISING GENERATION OF COACHMEN:

TO THOSE

'CHIPS OF THE OLD BLOCK'

WHO ASPIRE TO THE REKINDLING OF

'THE LIGHT OF OTHER DAYS:'

AND WITH BEST WISHES FOR THEIR SUCCESS

THIS VOLUME IS DEDICATED

BY

C. T. S. BIRCH REYNARDSON

INTRODUCTION.

IN THESE DAYS of revived Coaching, when there seems
to be a perfect mania amongst the young men of the
present day for a trip 'down the Road,' and when
the Park is enlivened by so many 'aspirants to the
whip,' with their smart coaches and gaudy-going
high-stepping teams, I trust I shall not be thought
presumptuous in offering a sketch and a few anecdotes of old times to the young Coaching British
Public. My coaching days are over ; but as the
worn-out charger neighs at the sound of the trumpet,
as the old huntsman revives at the crack of the whip
and the sound of the horn, so do I, when I see or
hear of a coach, call back the days when coaches
were in their glory. 'The light of other days' has
faded, it is true, but still there are some remaining
who can recall with pleasure the 'palmy days of old.'

There are few, very few, now remaining, I fear, who have really worked a coach by night and by day, through wind and rain, frost and snow, and who have really done the thing in rough and smooth.

If there should be any of the old ones left to read my humble production, they will, I think, bear me out that, pleasant as it was, it was on many occasions hard work, and at times not quite devoid of danger and a considerable amount of responsibility.

In producing my 'Reminiscences' I wish to afford amusement to those of the present day, and to tell them how their poor old governors or their poor dear old grandpapas used to see and hear things now for ever past and gone. I wish I had either the pen or wit of a Whyte Melville or of a Wilkie Collins to put all I wish to say into better language, and to describe the incidents of the Road in a more 'juicy' way. But not having either their pen or their wit, I must ask my readers to be what is termed 'kind readers,' and to be indulgent. I daresay some will take delight in picking 'my work' to pieces; but when they consider that though educated at Eton I did not learn much there but mischief, and that though my education was supposed to be finished at Cambridge I did not learn much there but to drive coaches, they must not expect to get water out of an empty pitcher.

TO THE READER.

—◦◦—

READER, whilst you whisk along in your cosy first-
class carriage to Scotland, by the express, on that
best of all lines, the Great Northern, doing your forty
miles, or even more, an hour, with your comfortable
foot-warmer, the 'Times' in your hand, and probably
your pipe in your mouth, does it ever enter your
head that the 400 miles that it takes you ten hours,
or even less, to accomplish, were not performed under
two days and two nights by your old father, or even
in a longer time by 'poor dear old grandpapa,' who
considered that a railroad was an invention of the
devil, and who declared that he would never do anything but post if railways were permitted to travel
at a greater rate than fifteen miles an hour? Does
it ever occur to you that whilst you are rattling
along at such a pace, and feeling so secure and cosy

in your snug corner of the carriage, the pointsman, a
mile ahead of you, may, for some cause or unforeseen
accident—possibly from the water in his tea having been
too strong—have neglected to attend to his points, and
that you are on the high road to the coal-train, which
has just shunted to let you pass ; or that you are,
without the least possible chance or means of avoiding
it, well into the cattle-train, which is making all play
to get away from the down express, and for which it
ought to shunt at the next station ? No wonder that
your 'poor dear old grandpapa' should rather post
than subject himself to such terrors, the bare thoughts
of which are enough to cause him a terrible nightmare. 'Ah!' he would sometimes say, 'it was very
dangerous travelling by a stage-coach, or even by a
post-chaise, particularly if there were four horses ; for
if the postboys got drunk, which they often did, there
was a great danger of being upset. A stage-coach,
too, was often very heavily loaded ; and if two coaches
were what they used to call "opposition coaches,"
they used to race one against the other, and gallop

along the road, and swing about in a most dangerous manner; and when this was the case they sometimes got turned over, and the passengers used to get hurt. There was danger in travelling by a coach, but, after all, nothing to a railway. You got upset in a coach or in a chaise, and there you were. You get upset in a railway, and where are you?' so said poor dear old grandpapa.

But you are very comfortable in your corner. Your 'Times' is, luckily for you, fairly clear as to print this morning, which, by the way, is not an everyday occurrence; your pipe draws well, which it very often does not; your tobacco is good, which it generally is, for it is Simmons' Mixture, of 62, Piccadilly—not quite worth fourteen shillings a pound, I should say; but that is his price, and good things, they say, always fetch their value. Your thoughts turn to the pace you are going, and how merrily you slip along; you pass through the country as if you were riding a whirl-wind; you pass villages, and churches, and houses, and fields, and fences, and can hardly distinguish

them ; your only object is to get over the ground ;
you are on your way to Edinburgh, and you are in
the ' Rusher.' Well, you say to yourself, I wonder
how my governor could ever get through his time outside a coach ; how deuced cold, too, he must have
been on such a day as this ; and as to ' poor dear old
grandpapa,' I don't wonder that he's used up and done
for, if they travelled still slower in his days than they
did in the governor's. Such thoughts, perhaps, pass
in your mind, and it is to you that I shall offer a few
anecdotes of olden times,—tales of old coaching days
along the old North Road, the old Holyhead Road,
and other roads that in my early days I have fre-
quented, and upon which it has delighted me ' Col-
legisse pulverem Olympicum.'

The anecdotes have all come under my own obser-
vation, and therefore I may be thought to be always
talking and telling of myself. If I do appear thus
egotistical, do not be too hard upon me. What I have
noted down are real facts ; and if, when you have
finished reading your ' Times,' and have lit another

pipe 'Reminiscences of a Gentleman Coachman' help
to beguile your time till you come into collision with
either of the trains I have before named, the little
effort I have made to amuse you and the object I
have had in view will be fully attained by me.

There cannot be many in 1874 who have been
on a coach so long since as 1823 or 1824. There
may be some; but, alas! how few remain to tell
the tale. There may be some few remaining, but
time has thinned their ranks, and those who do remain must, according to the rules of 'Anno Domini,'
be old men. Fifty, or even forty, years is a long
time to look back upon, it is true; but in reality
the time has flown away with incredible rapidity, and
days and weeks and years have, as it were, travelled
by an express train. I am one of the 'old ones' that
remain, and from that fact, and the fact of having
always had a *penchant* for 'the Road,' I have seen
many things happen during the last fifty years that
cannot by any means take place again. 'Tempora
mutantur, nos et mutamur in illis,' as the poet has

it. Since those days men are changed, coaches are changed, horses are changed, and the very *modus operandi* seems changed. There is no real ' Down the Road' in the present day; and a real old mail and the real old stage-coach, with its piles of luggage and all other etceteras, should, before every recollection of them is gone, have a place, fully equipped for the Road as in times of old, in the British Museum. It would not be a bad thought for some enterprising old ' Down the Road' to set the thing on foot, and thus hand down to posterity what would be a wonder to behold when the generation to come travel by electricity instead of steam.

The incidents and anecdotes which will appear in my book were not originally written for publication. For the amusement of those of tenderer years than myself who showed a tendency to follow in the steps of 'a worn-out coachman,' I used sometimes to relate some of my stories, and on many occasions I have had it said to me, ' Why don't you publish them ? They would make a capital book to read on the railroad.' I have at length put many little facts together, and, with the wish to afford amusement to others, I have tried to describe some of the incidents which used to take place in years now long past and gone, but the memory of which still clings on.

> You may break, you may ruin the vase if you will,
> But the scent of the roses will hang round it still.

So says Tom Moore. 'Quo semel est imbuta recens, servabit odorem testa diu,' says our old friend Horace, who is another and a greater authority. It is hard to forget the joyous days of old; and though I and others of my contemporaries are, like the vase, broken and ruined by 'Anno Domini,' still—

> Sunt quos curriculo pulverem Olympicum
> Collegisse juvat.

And to them, with their permission, and asking their kind indulgence, I beg to dedicate

DOWN THE ROAD

OR

REMINISCENCES OF A GENTLEMAN COACHMAN.

b

CONTENTS.

	PAGE
INTRODUCTION	vii
TO THE READER	xi
ROAD VERSUS RAIL	1
THE OLD MAIL HORN	8
CHARTER HOUSE DAYS .	10
COLLEGE DAYS	17
'REGENT' COACH	33
THE 'PEACOCK' AT ISLINGTON .	43
WELLYN HILL AND OLD BARKER	49
THE CROOKED WHIP AND TOM HENNESY	54
TOM HENNESY'S ACCOMPLISHMENTS	60
THE SIX HILLS AT STEVENAGE .	63
THE ROAD GAME	65
TOM HENNESY REDUCED TO A PAIR	67
THE WORLD CAN'T GET ON WITHOUT HUMBUG .	71

		PAGE
KITES OVER MONCKS WOOD		76
THE LOUTH MAIL .		78
I GO TO LIVE NEAR THE HOLYHEAD ROAD		80
THE HOLYHEAD MAIL FROM LONDON VIÂ SHREWSBURY		83
OGWYN POOL	.	87
HOLYHEAD MAIL		96
THREE BLIND 'UNS AND A BOLTER .		102
THE LITTLE FAST TEAM FROM THE RISING SUN		109
JACK WILLIAMS' RECOMMENDATION OF AN INN		112
HODGSON WON'T READ MY PARCELS		114
WHEELER WITHOUT HARNESS		117
DICK VICKERS .		119
HARRY JONES ASKS ME TO DRIVE THE 'BUS OVER THE MENAI BRIDGE .	.	125
MAIL.—CHESTER AND HOLYHEAD .	.	128
'SALL I STAMP THE FOOTBOARD?'		135
CRUELTY TO DUMB ANIMALS .	. .	138
THE ST. GOTHARD PASS		141
MOPING A HOT LEADER .		150
NETTLE COACH		153
THE PIG AT LLANYMYNECK TOLL-BAR .		155
'PETER HILTON' AND THE STRANGE GENTLEMAN .		160

	PAGE
THE REASON WHY HORSES GO BETTER AT NIGHT	165
'THE LODGE HILL'	168
THE STAGE COACH OF OLD, AND THE LOAD IT USED TO CARRY	179
SMALL HINTS THAT MAY BE USEFUL	183
THE AMATEUR 'SHOOTER'	199
HOW JOHN BARKER STARTS A REFRACTORY TEAM	201
ALWAYS GO ROUND YOUR HORSES	203
MIND THAT THE TOLL-BAR MAN DON'T SHUT THE GATE IN YOUR FACE	205
AN OLD COACHMAN	208
FAREWELL TO THE READER	216
ALAS! ALAS! WHERE IS IT GONE?	219
POSTSCRIPT	221

LIST OF PLATES.

——◆——

SCENE ON THE DOVER ROAD	*Frontispiece*	
SUNRISE	*To face p.*	1
'HARRY! OFFSIDE LEADER'S TRACE UNHOOKED!' . .	,,	33
TOM AND I SLIP INTO 'THE BAR'	,,	56
TOM HENNESY'S CROOKED WHIP.	,,	59
'WHAT! DRUNK AGAIN, YOU LAZY OLD BEGGAR?'	,,	79
BICKNELL'S SPICY TEAM OF GREYS	,,	95
OUR FRIEND IN RED KEEPS HIS HORN GOING	,,	128
A STICKY LOT.	,,	136
A STIFFISH PITCH, BUT A GOOD TEAM	,,	138
NEAR-SIDE, JOE. TRACE GONE AGAIN!	,,	185
A CHEERY LOOK-OUT	,,	209

'DOWN THE ROAD.'

ROAD VERSUS RAIL.

It has often been a subject of wonder to me that no one has ever written any sort of book relating to Coaching or incidents of the Road in times gone by, and I am well aware that so humble a pen as mine cannot set forth in a proper way the incidents I should wish to describe. In the present mode of travelling, comfortable and expeditious as it may be, there is little of the amusement there formerly was on the Road. Everybody now seems to be in a hurry, everybody seems to wish to be first, and everybody does the best he can, and takes the quickest means to get to his journey's end.

The tea-kettle, with its steam, has taken the place of the four bright bays; the grimy engine-driver and stoker have taken the place of the coachman; the

guard or conductor in his blue coat and foreign-look-
ing cap, has taken the place of the guard in red, with
his glazed hat and cockade; and the long mellow
horn of former days is now replaced by a shrill and
certainly not to be called mellow whistle. The railway
carriage, it is true, is a large, commodious affair, with
its comfortable padded seats, windows that fit tight,
a lamp in the roof to turn darkness into light in the
tunnels through which the train passes as it speeds
on its headlong way through the bowels of the earth.
A comfortable foot-warmer of tin or zinc filled with
hot water warms the feet of the old ladies and gentlemen, and even of young ladies and young gentlemen,
and of little boys returning home for their holidays,
or with saddened hearts going back to school. How
different is all this from former days, when the stage
coach, with its four in and twelve out, or the mail,
with its four in and three outside, exclusive of the
coachman and guard, started upon its journey of perhaps three or four hundred miles at eight o'clock
at night, or at, let us say, six o'clock in the morning!
The snow is on the ground, the wind blowing pierc-
ingly cold, for it also freezes hard, the stars shining

SIX O'CLOCK IN THE MORNING
From London.

THE PROPRIETORS OF

THE REGENT COACH

Respectfully inform the public and their friends in particular, that, for their more *perfect convenience*, and to keep pace with the daily improvements in travelling, *the hour of its leaving London will be altered* on Monday the 13th of May, (and continued during the summer months,)

TO SIX O'CLOCK IN THE MORNING,
Instead of Night.

The arrangements that are forming in furtherance of this long-desired alteration, will ensure a steady and punctual conveyance of Passengers to Stamford by a Quarter before Six o'clock, and to Melton by a Quarter before Nine o'clock in the Evening.

The hours of leaving Melton and Stamford will NOT be altered.

The proprietors take this opportunity to acknowledge their sense of the decided patronage shown to the Regent Coach under their several regulations, and to repeat their promise that no exertion shall be wanting to make it one of the most desirable conveyances to and from London.

Passengers and Parcels booked at Mr. Weldon's, and the Bull and Swan Inn, Stamford; and at Mr. Sharpe's, Bell Inn, Melton. *Stamford, May* 1, 1822.

Drakard.

NOTICE.

This Coach leaves London at Six o'clock in the Morning.

From the George and Blue Boar, Holborn.

brighter than the brightest diamonds, and the morning, except for the light of the stars, as dark as pitch.
It is six o'clock A.M., as they say in these days, in the
month of February 1824, and no chance of reaching
the 'George and Blue Boar,' Holborn, before nine or
ten o'clock at night—a pretty look out for the three little
boys who are now mounting on to the 'Regent' coach
at Stamford on their way back to school, wrapped in
their long drab great-coats. The coach is piled up
with luggage till it is loaded like a stage-waggon, and
one only wonders how such a heavily loaded conveyance ever reached its destination without breaking
down or being upset.

The three little fellows have mounted up to their
seats on the roof of the coach, and, though they have
been told by their anxious parents to be sure and go
inside, persist in going, one on the box with the coachman, and the other two behind him, and declare man-
fully that they are not cold and never feel the cold.
They have each got some straw; not new straw, for
that is cold stuff, but straw out of the stables which
has been a little used and trampled by the horses; and
having shoved their little feet into it, instead of on to a

hot foot-warmer, as in the present day, feel as cheery as possible.

The boy of the present day has no idea of what his father, or perhaps I might better say his poor dear old grandpapa, suffered on his journey from six o'clock A.M. till his arrival at nine or ten o'clock P.M. at the 'George and Blue Boar,' Holborn, on such a morning as I have tried to describe, which albeit was a fine morning for the time of year, for there was no snow actually falling, nor was there any rain, as often was the case, to melt the snow and make everything sloppy and miserable—raining down from six in the morning till the arrival of the coach at nine at night; raining down without intermission till coats, hats, and one's very flesh were wet through to the bone.

It was indeed misery, or next door to it; but still all were kept alive and in something like a merry mood by the incidents on the road.

The coachman was generally a good-natured kind of fellow, and had his jokes with every one along the road, in spite of either cold or wet.

The guard too was usually a cheery fellow, and often played the keyed bugle well, or, if on the mail, cheered one up with the sound of his 'mellow horn,' often called his 'yard of tin,' for in old times it was made of tin, and was about a yard long. Such was the travelling in former days. The pace now no doubt is greater, the comfort is greater; but with all this the fun and interest, as well as the incidents, of the road are gone for ever.

The three little boys in their long drab great-coats are now old men; and, according to the traditions of the Pawnee Indian, are awaiting their turn to go to those happy hunting grounds where it is supposed by them that those who deserve to be happy will find 'the light of other days' unfaded and bright as in days of old.

The coachmen are dead—the guards are dead. 'Trumpeter unus erat, coatum qui scarlet habebat,' he is dead; and his Mail Horn's sound is heard no more.

THE OLD MAIL HORN.

THE horn that once upon the mail
  Its soul of music shed,
Now hangs all mute against the wall
  And tells of guards long dead;
So sleeps the horn of former years,
  Its stirring sounds are o'er,
And toll-bar men and horsekeepers
  Now hear that sound no more.

No more to roadside inns, alas!
  The mail horn's music swells;
No more upon the midnight breeze
  The mail's arrival tells;
The drowsy passenger ne'er wakes,
  Roused by that midnight horn;
That sound is dead and never breaks
  The still of the early morn.

But shall these sounds be quite forgot.
  Though guards are past and gone?
There still remain some hearts that loved
  The sound of that mellow horn;
And though the coachmen of old are dead,
  Though the guards are turned to clay,
There are those who remember the ' Yard of Tin,'
  And the mail of the olden day.

THE OLD MAIL HORN.

Either of the lines may be sounded.   Any other notes are wrong, and, indeed, impossible.

CHARTER HOUSE DAYS.

JOHN BARKER.—MY FIRST TEAM.

I WAS a very little fellow when I first took the notion that I should like to be able to drive. As far as my memory serves me, it was in the year of grace 1823 or 1824, when I was a little chap at that horrible of all horrible places called a 'seat of learning,' the 'Charter House.' In those days it was a regular prison, and in the dirtiest part of London, and close to Smithfield. The unfortunate boys never wore hats, went bareheaded, and generally looked as if their fathers must have been chimney-sweeps. In winter, as a general rule, the playground was some inches deep in black sludge. Wet through and cold as we often were, such a thing as a change of raiment was unknown. There were always a lot of big bullies who would not let a poor little wretch warm himself at the fire; and, if they caught you there, the chances were they half roasted you, which was performed by toasting your miserable little

'Hinder end' before the fire, till it was too hot for *manipulation*, and then scraping it down with a Latin or Greek grammar, or with that more important work called a 'Gradus.' After having been bullied and knocked about, roasted and toasted, tossed in a blanket till I touched the ceiling and burst a hole through the blanket, and was nearly killed by coming in contact with the floor of the long bedroom in which some eight or ten of us slept, I was taken home very ill and was supposed to be going to die.

This, however, I did not do ; and, much to my de-light, was taken away from the horrible prison and sent to that seat of sound learning and religious education called Eton. 'Floreat Etona' is its motto, and I be-lieve no one who was educated there has ever regretted that part of his education.

As I travelled to and from school I made up my mind that there was nothing like a coach and four horses, and the idea of being some day able to drive four horses was the height of my ambition. I believe I used to dream of the coach and horses and the old fat coachman into whose charge I used to be given at Stamford, and by whose side I used always to have that dignified situation, 'the box-seat.' He was a good, kind old man, nearly as big as Daniel Lambert; a good, though not at all a swell coachman, but strong as the 'mighty man of Gath,' and as safe as the bank.

I well remember it was quite a privilege to be allowed to unbuckle his reins as he got within a few yards of his change.

He drove the 'Regent' coach, which ran from Stamford to London for many years. He was the first man that ever put reins into my hand, and seemed to take a pride in teaching me the 'gentle art.' I had therefore a great regard for him. He hurt his foot in getting off the coach one day, and things went wrong with him. After a time mortification set in, and he died, regretted by all who knew him. Poor old John Barker, for that was his name, 'requiescit in pace' in St. Michael's churchyard at Stamford, from which town he had driven to Huntingdon pretty nearly every day but Sunday for more than twenty years.

The 'Regent,' though not a fast coach, was always well horsed by Mr. Whincup of the 'George Hotel' at Stamford.

My First Team.

Well do I remember my first attempt to drive, and well do I remember my father's horror at seeing me seated as high as I could pile cushions on the seat of a low two-wheeled sort of gig, which was something more extraordinary in shape than anything I can describe. It was not like a gig ; but still it was a gig, for it had a pair of shafts and two wheels. I might almost say it was like a green garden-chair to hold two, on wheels, or like a very roomy wheelbarrow ; but, as a wheelbarrow has only one wheel, it could not be quite like that article. But it was so curious a looking machine that it might have been a hybrid between a garden-chair and a wheelbarrow. Be that as it may, to this nondescript conveyance, after much ingenuity, I had harnessed two donkeys, tandem fashion, and had constructed a whip from an old gig whip and some old thongs I had found with various other odds and ends in an old drawer of my father's, which abounded with rubbish of all sorts, my father having in his day, like myself in my day, a great propensity for rubbish, feeling, I daresay, as I do, that everything or anything may come into use

some day, though one never knows when that day may
be. Thus equipped, I started on my first attempt to be
a follower of Jehu. I don't know that I exactly wanted
to meet my father, who was gone out riding with his old
friend, Dr. Willis. I felt pretty sure I would rather not
meet them, and I also felt pretty certain that I should not
meet them. So off I started, if going from one side of
the road to the other could be called starting. Nevertheless, it was the best start I could make ; and except
that my leader persisted in turning round and looking me
full in the face, and seemed to threaten to sit beside me,
we got on pretty well, considering the sort of team I had
to deal with ; for, be it known to all men, ' Balaam ' is by
no means a ' canny beast' if he takes it into his head to
be ' uncanny.'

Well, I felt proud of my performance altogether,
and was paying away, first at my wheeler and then
at my leader, to the best of my ability ; and the
more I payed away the more they seemed to want
paying ; and were very like lawyers, who every one
knows do nothing without being paid. All of a sudden,
who should appear round a corner in the road but
my father and his friend ! I was horror-struck ; and

so I suppose was he, for he at once exclaimed :—
' Hallo! what the deuce have we got here? why
Charles, what are you up to ? surely you don't want
to learn to be a coachman ? and trying to drive a
tandem, too! Of all things in the world a tandem is
the most dangerous, and the most slang. I never saw
a tandem in my life that I did not expect to see the
leader turn into a mad-house!' This to be sure was
rather 'talking shop,' as it so happened that Dr. Willis
kept a private mad-house, or what is called a ' crazy
shop ;' and I daresay that they both thought that I
was a fit subject for bed and board in that then well-
known establishment, which was about seven miles
from the spot where the rencontre took place. My
father, however, was more amused than vexed, said
that I was a foolish fellow, and that, though he liked
my being fond of riding, he did not care about my
learning to be a coachman ; for he had a horror of a
gentleman coachman, and thought that every man
that drove a coach and four must keep company with
coachmen, use slang terms, drink brandy and water,
be able to swear like a moss-trooper, and have a
tooth knocked out to spit through. Therefore, as I,

like every other little cypher, had my own immediate
circle of admiring relatives, he naturally did not wish
to see his son become a blackguard ; and, as I was his
eldest son, he thought the propensity I was showing
to become a disciple of Jehu one that might bring
disgrace upon his house, which was a house much
given to hunting and equitation of all kinds, but not
in its remotest time in any way given to the coaching
business.   My father, himself, was a first-rate man on
a horse, a first-rate judge of a horse, had a first-rate
seat on a horse, and the best hand on a horse that
I ever knew ; but on wheels he was not in his element.
He did not care about driving ; he was quite innocent
of this 'gentle art ;' and, high as my opinion of him
was in everything appertaining to horse flesh, I used
always to ʻsee fearʼ if he by chance drove me even
in a gig ; and as to sitting beside him in anything like
a tandem, or with four horses—a performance which
there is no tradition of his having ever attempted—I
would rather have gone up in a balloon, which is a
thing of which I have more horror than anything
else.

Oh ! when I was at College, oh !
Oh ! when I was at College, oh !
When I was there
Of leaves quite bare
I stript the tree of knowledge, oh !

At least so I conclude my anxious parents thought I should. I had, however, no pretensions to the kind of thing. I never was fond of Greek and Latin; and, though I had had a certain amount of it knocked into me at Eton and elsewhere, I never could see the fun of it; and when I was made aware that my destination was to be Trinity College, Cambridge, I must own I did not quite relish the thoughts of going to school again, for I must make my readers aware that I was intended for quite a different profession, and when I left Eton I was to go into the Guards— a thing that I remember Dr. Keate, of immortal memory, who was in those days the Head Master at Eton, did not at all approve of for me. On 'taking leave' I slipped into his hand the usual tip of a

11

ten-pound note (a horrid custom and abuse it was),
which, by the way, he opened and looked at in
my presence, fearing, I suppose, that I might have
given him merely a bit of silver paper—a trick
once played on him. Wishing me all good luck,
he begged to know what I was going to do in
the way of a profession. On my telling him that I
was going 'into the Guards,' he said, ' I am very sorry
for it; I am very sorry to hear it; it's a very bad
school; but I wish you well. Good-bye!' Why or
wherefore I know not, but the dear, good old man
had an intense horror of a soldier, and most particularly of a Guardsman. How he used to 'swish'
a fellow if he caught him up at barracks! what a
mortal hatred he had to the very name of barracks!
It was two rods and fourteen cuts, at the very least,
if you got reported for being 'up at barracks;' and
I dare say that there are still those living who have
taken the same without flinching, and who will bear
me out in what I have said. I have never received
it myself, but I have seen it administered more than
once, for this heinous offence. It used to be the
fashion to say that flogging did not hurt; but as far

as my experience goes it did hurt most deucedly. Seven cuts for ordinary offences with a new rod with plenty of buds on it I have often had, and it used to be quite sharp enough to please *me*; but double that dose must have been rather hard to swallow without making wry faces. I have, however, often seen a fellow take it with as much 'sang froid' as if he had been made of leather or gutta-percha.

There may be some antiquated Etonians, like myself, still remaining, who may read this, and they, like myself, may have 'come under the lash' of the dear old Dr. Keate. I say 'the dear old Dr. Keate,' because 'Old Keate,' as we used to call him then, was a good, kind old man by nature, quite a character in his way, and withal a most impartial one. He would 'swish' a lord with quite as much 'gusto' as he 'swished' a commoner; and the little, dirty, unwashed, mutton-eating 'tug' fared, I sometimes used to think, better than the dapper, clean, little embryo lord, or aspirant to a coronet, who stood in the rank of condemned criminals, 'Metuens pendentis habenæ,' in a row of eight or ten, or sometimes even twenty, all ready to answer to their names, and step up to the

block on which they had to kneel, and suffer the
penalty of the law, according to their precedence in
the school or the heinousness of their crime. Verily
it was a goodly sight in those olden days to see ten·
or twenty of England's sons standing in a row, with
their nether garments down, and a smile on their
face, awaiting their doom, and ready to shed their
blood in the cause of idleness or mischief, and prepared
to take without a sound or murmur whatever the 'dear
old Doctor' might be pleased to administer to them.
'You Lord A. here again,' he would say, 'for having
been seen coming out of barracks by Mr. Oakes! and
you R. for having been complained of by your Dame
for calling her bad names. I shall flog you both very
severely; you are both of you a disgrace to the school,
a burden to your parents, and a misery to yourselves.'

    As our dear friend Horace used to say, 'Pallida
Mors' was no respecter of persons, so it was with
poor dear old Keate; high or low, rich or poor,
gentle or simple, it was all the same; he gave it us
all round, whether we deserved it or not, if we were
in the black list and found standing in that condemned row; and I verily believe the good little man

rather enjoyed the operation, whatever his patients might have thought of the matter. But I am almost 'off the road.' I could not, however, as an old Etonian, refrain from paying a slight tribute of respect to one who was, beyond a doubt, the best Whip of his day—the time I am speaking of being from about 1824 to 1828.

To cut matters short, having met with a bad accident, and having injured my hip, I had to give up all thoughts of soldiering, and, after much not knowing what to do with me, I was sent to Cambridge. When I had limped about on crutches for two or three years, Trinity College, Cambridge, became my destination. On arriving there, I found that the greater part of my Eton contemporaries had left; they had either taken their degrees, or been plucked, or had left, or had gone somewhere or another; still there remained a few of the old familiar faces of Eton days to greet me.

'Hallo! old fellow,' said B—hr—d, 'what! are you come up? Why, we are all leaving; you'll know no-body here. I suppose you're not come up to read, are you?' 'No!' said I, with a decided emphasis; 'certainly not. How could you ask such a question?' He

knew my aversion to anything of the kind, and, having
been nearly next to me at Eton for four years, he had
no business to ask me. 'Well, then,' said he, 'I'll give
you a little bit of very useful advice, if you'll conde-
scend to take it. Don't you go to anything till you are
told, except to Hall. You must go to Hall to get
marked in, or you'll lose your term ; don't go to anything else till you're told, or sent for. Some of the
dons will soon send for you to ask you why you have
not been to lectures and chapels, and so forth; it will
be all in good time for you to go then.' To this piece
of advice I religiously adhered, and pleaded ignorance of
all the duties expected of me till I was sent for, which,
you may suppose, soon came to pass. I really am
almost ashamed to tell you, good reader, by what arti-
fices I got out of lectures, chapels, and everything I
ought to have done ; but I started on my friend's advice,
and taking for my motto, 'Vestigia nulla retrorsum,' I
went boldly on, and succeeded better than I could possibly have anticipated. To go to chapel on an empty
stomach, at seven o'clock in the morning, was what I
positively could not do, and, the more I digested the
matter, the more I made up my mind I would not do.

Besides, the Stamford and Leicester coach used to start at seven, and I did not see how I could possibly be in chapel and driving the said coach at the same time. It was therefore decided that I could not go to chapel. I was sent for by the Dean, who said that he was very sorry to find that I did not attend chapel, and so forth ; he was really very courteous, and I soon began to find that I had got on the 'soft side' of him. Of course, I made the best running that I could under such propitious circumstances ; and at last, having used the most persuasive eloquence that I possessed, I got him to agree with me, that being lame, and walking with *two* sticks, I might possibly slip and hurt myself on the slippery marble pavement of which the floor of the chapel was composed. I always walked with two sticks when in College ; but I almost fancy that when away from that seat of learning, and when out of the sight of dons and tutors, I managed pretty well with only one. I must not, however, hurt your feelings with the relation of all that took place to enable me to get out of the attendance at chapel ; it would also be too much for my feelings to be obliged to rake up all the little 'ruses' I was obliged to employ for that purpose. Suffice it to say, that the Dean most considerately excused me all chapels; and, though I often went at that time to drive the coach, I used to console myself in reflecting whether I was not quite as well employed in learning so useful a trade, as those who were forced to attend in a sacred place when their hearts were anywhere but there.

I don't think that there was a vast deal of life on the Stamford coach, which went through Stamford to Leicester; certainly not so much as on many others. The coachman, John Hennesy, or 'Saddler Jack,' as he used to be called, was not by any means a lively or amusing fellow, and there was nothing particularly lively about the whole turnout; but it was a convenient coach for a drive down to Stamford and back again in the evening. The Cambridge men made a good deal of use of it to go to some of the meets of the Fitzwilliam Hounds; and, as one learnt to drive, that was a profitable and useful occupation whilst 'up at Cambridge.' I don't know whether my father thought so when I drove up to the 'George' Inn door one day when he happened to be in Stamford, from which place he lived about seven miles; but, as he did not say

much, I suppose he thought that it was all right, and
that it might be part of the education I was going
through at the University.

I remember one day, as I was going through Stamford, on my way from home, where I had been for a
couple of days on leave, I had brought a whip with
me to drive the coach back to Cambridge. I was in
a high kind of dog-cart; and, as I turned the corner of
St. Mary's Churchyard, a young sparrow was sitting on
a grave-stone within reach of me, fluttering his wings
and soliciting grub from his parents. The temptation
was too great to be resisted. I opened my thong, gave
it a couple of twists round, let drive at him, and cut
his head as clean off his shoulders as if it had been
done with a pair of scissors.

The whip with which I performed this feat—rather
a cruel one, perhaps—came to a sad and curious end.
I had broken the thong, and, being a pet stick, I used
it for a time as a gig-whip. It was standing in the
socket of my gig at the door of the 'Peacock' Inn, at
Boston, in Lincolnshire. My groom was waiting for
me near my gig, larking and making insinuating faces
at the chambermaid, who was in a room above. He

caught sight of me, and as he turned his back she heaved a feather-bed out of the window at him, which, horrible to relate, fell on the top of my whip, and of course you can judge what happened.

I GO TO ELY CATHEDRAL IN A TANDEM.

I HAD not much coaching whilst at Cambridge, except on the coach I have before named, running through Stamford to Leicester; but sometimes I used to drive one of those most dangerous of all turnsout, called a tandem. There is no safety in the turnout unless you take a blunderbuss with you to shoot your leader dead upon the spot the moment he turns round and looks you in the face, which he can do at any moment he likes. The only chance you have, if you are not provided with the firearm I have named, is being very handy with your whip, and cobbing him across the eyes and ears to turn him round again, if possible; for if your leader does not choose to go straight of his own accord, you might just as well try to drive an eel or the great sea-serpent. However, I was rash enough at times to peril my own life and that of others in that conveyance, and was particularly fond of getting a man who wanted to go somewhere, who would pay half the expenses, and who did not want to drive. I will now describe a drive from Cambridge to Ely to see the Cathedral, and the view from the top of it, with a friend who at the time little dreamt of the fate that awaited him in after years, in what was supposed to be a much safer conveyance—no more or less than the Irish Limited Mail. Poor John Aylmer! he was burnt to death with Lord Farnham and others in that dire accident near Abergele, on the Holyhead Line, when the train was set on fire by the explosion of some casks of petroleum. The accident is too well known for me to dwell upon it here.

A kind, good fellow he was in olden days, and often have I thought of his sad and terrible end as I have passed the spot. I had lost sight of him for many years, from my having been much abroad since my College days; but the circumstance of passing the spot where such a scene had happened never failed to bring the old friend of former days to my mind. Poor John Aylmer! We started together one very fine, bright day from Cambridge to see the view from the

top of Ely Cathedral; he paid half the expenses of
the tandem, and, not caring about driving, I drove,
which just suited me; and I was to stand luncheon
at 'the Inn,' as it was called in those days. After
much puffing and blowing, I managed to get to the top
of the tower of the Cathedral, and was leaning against
the wall mopping my head and face, for it was a
piping hot day I well remember, when on turning
round whom should I meet face to face but the
Reverend William Whewell, who was commonly called
by us in College 'Billy Whistle.' There was no
evading him, and therefore brass and assurance were
the only things left. Now, as I never possessed either
of these invaluable commodities, you may suppose that
I was in a bit of a fix. 'Well, I am surprised to
see you here, Mr. Reynardson,' said the worthy Billy.
'Indeed, sir,' said I, 'you cannot be more surprised
to see me here, than I am to find myself here. I
have been over-persuaded by my friend, Mr. Aylmer,
to come and see the view, and with the assistance of
my stick and his arm I have managed to get up, but
how I shall ever get down again I don't know. The
wish to see the fine view has tempted me to do more

than is prudent, I am afraid.' ' Indeed, I think it very praiseworthy of you to make an effort to see such a view,' said he ; 'and when you wish to go down again, I shall be very happy to lend you an arm if it will be of any use to you.' This he did most kindly, and the great ' Billy Whistle ' and I got safely to the bottom, when he congratulated me on my safe descent, and we parted. I never after heard of having been seen at that high elevation, though I was, as before, excused all chapels from being lame. I had as much right to be on the top of Ely Cathedral as my friend Billy, but it was rather an exalted position for a man who could not walk without two sticks when in College ! The reverend dignitary would not have been very much pleased had he understood what was going on ; but, as he did not, he was most kind and affable, which he often was not. If his coat was brushed at all the wrong way, he could be very three-cornered and unpleasant indeed.

I remember on another occasion having driven a friend over to Huntingdon. On our return, rather late in the evening, our lamps went out, and when near the toll-bar, pretty close to Cambridge, where we always took our leader off for fear of being seen and 'nailed' by any of the authorities, it was so dark that I could see neither horses, nor road, nor anything else. All of a sudden we came to a dead stand. It was as dark as the inside of a railway carriage without a lamp in a tunnel. I could see nothing, and could not imagine what had happened. 'Just nip down, B.,' said I, 'and see if you can make out where we are, and what is up. I almost fancy that we must be off the road altogether.' After some little investigation of how matters stood, B. broke out into a laugh, and said, 'No wonder you can't make out where you are ; you're right off the road, and the little Chestnut is sitting in the ditch.' I remember as well as if it were yesterday that my team consisted of two horses belonging to a man of the name of Nun, and went by the names of 'Old

Thurnwell' and 'Nun's little Chestnut.' The latter, I think, showed great good sense in sitting down, instead of turning the whole affair over into the ditch.

A real tandem cart, such as I was then driving, is never seen in these days; and as perhaps not one in a thousand, if so many there be who read this, has ever dreamt of so dangerous a conveyance, I will try to describe it; for, dangerous as it was, a really well turned out tandem, painted chocolate and picked out with lake, was a neat and 'varmint'-looking affair, and, as long as all went right, pleasant to 'ride' upon; but if anything went wrong, if your wheeler came down, or any such mishap took place, you got such a 'father and mother of a fall' as it is out of my power to describe.

The tandem cart was thus, a sort of gig on very high wheels, with a square body and a seat behind, like a mail guard's, or that on a hansom cab of the present day, quite straight shafts and a foot-board well above your wheeler's back, no dashing leather of any kind; in fact, it was like sitting on the box of a low drag. A mighty dangerous concern, no doubt; but I suppose there was an extra excitement in driving a

carriage more likely than any other conveyance I can
name to come to grief and go to smash at a moment's
notice.   So now, good reader, as I have put you on
your box, and given you proper caution, remember
that you have only two wheels, that you are up
pretty high, and that if you do come down 'you'll
come down with a run,' and very possibly and very
probably, like ' Humpty Dumpty' of great renown, will
never get up again.

Perils by Water.

THERE were various modes of being made nervous on a coach, and I do not think anything made one's heart come into one's mouth much more than having to go through water. On the 'Regent' coach we used to leave the main road, at times, and go round by the St. Neot's paper mills, which were situated on a flat piece of ground, and occasionally, when the weather had been what the Scotchman calls 'varra saft' for any length of time, the river Ouse would take it into its head to overflow its banks, and lay the road for about half a mile under water. Upon those occasions we often had a pair of leaders put on which were ridden by a horsekeeper, not only to keep us in the right track, but to pull us through the mud and silt which made the road extra 'gummy.'

F

I have seen the water over the axle-trees; and on one occasion it fairly ran into the coach, and all but set afloat two old ladies who were inside. Their dismay may be easily imagined, and their supplications to the coachman to stop, as the water was coming into the coach, were quite affecting. They no doubt thought they were going to meet with a 'watery grave,' and I believe they gave themselves up as lost.

However, nothing so terrible took place ; but I have no doubt from the water having come over their shoes, and from their petticoats getting somewhat wet, they were not quite comfortable for the rest of their journey. We, on the outside, were nearly as much to be pitied, for it had rained without ceasing all day—that kind of pitiless rain which comes down straight, and in solid stripes, like the water from a shower-bath, which, in nautical language, goes by the appellation of 'raining marling-spikes with their points downwards;' the only difference between us and the old ladies being that whilst they got it from below we got it from above. It was nevertheless hardly to be called a pleasant state of things, to have water

above and water below, water on all sides, heaps of
stones by the roadside, invisible from the discoloured
water, and a deep ditch upon either side, into which
had one of our wheels gone, it would have been a
case of 'over you go, Jem Peck ; ' and all this with
the flood rising, so that it was all but impossible to
get on, and would be quite so in a few hours more.

Perils by Land.

Having described one little cause for nervousness
on a coach by water, I will mention one that occurred by land, and might have been another case of
'over you go, Jem Peck.' On the arrival of the
'Regent' coach at Wansford one fine summer's evening,
I remember the 'three little boys in their drab great-
coats' were returning home for their holidays from
Eton. We changed, as usual, at the 'Haycock' Inn,
kept by Mr. Percival. A very smart team of 'red
roans' was put in ; they were quite fit for any gentleman's drag, they were such a showy lot. 'Young
Percival,' as he was then called, got upon the box,
and, as his horses were pretty fresh, they did not

start quite kindly. He, being very full of valour and not quite as full of discretion, 'dropped into them,' which made matters worse, and they would not face the bridge, which every one who knows the 'North Road' is aware is a very awkward one, being very old and narrow, and anything but a bridge to play tricks upon. Just as we got to the bridge, what possessed the brutes I know not, but they whipped round all of a sudden, and after playing sundry antics—and a most nervous performance it was— we found ourselves at the door of the 'Haycock' Inn, from which we had just started, with our horses' heads pointing to London instead of to Stamford! How we got there safe, and without being turned over, neither I nor my two brothers, who were also on the coach, could ever make out. After the coach had been turned round again, under the Jehuship of 'Old John Barker,' we again faced the bridge, and arrived safely at Stamford. Nevertheless this was a case in which we ought to have been upset according to all the rules of accidents, and I may almost say of common sense. I well remember that 'Young Percival,' with most praise-

worthy pluck, proposed to 'tackle them' again ; but
' Old John' did not 'seem to see it,' and said, 'Come,
come, old friend; come, come, old friend; this will
never do; this will never do; you'll have us over;
I'm sure you would —I'm sure you'd have us over.'
And so after waiting a short time at the door, just to
give his horses time to come to their senses—which,
to a certain extent, they had lost in the 'skrimmage'
—we started afresh, and under his guidance surmounted the obstacle and got all right to our destination. It was a real touch-and-go business, and I only
wonder we were not all 'spilt.'

A Journey with Convicts from Chester Gaol, November 1834.

IT was not very often that one met with disagreeable company outside a coach, from the fact
that coaches did not usually carry the οἱ πολλοὶ and
the class of roughs that sometimes are to be seen in
these railroad days, in a third-class carriage, or in an
excursion train. The class of people that are now
to be seen making excursions everywhere, from the

Land's End to Johnny Groat's house, in the good
old times when 'the only steam came from the kettle,
stayed at home, and attended to their business, looked
more after their wives and families, and were less
inclined to roam than in these go-a-head days, for the
simple reason that they could not afford to 'ride,' and
therefore if they wanted to go any distance they had
to walk, or go by the stage-waggon or carrier's cart,
both of which were not only somewhat dearer than
walking, but quite as slow. There were, however, at
certain times a certain class of gentlemen who travelled at His Majesty's expense, and went under the
denomination of 'gaol birds.' Having once had the
pleasure of enjoying their agreeable society on a
coach, some notice of what took place upon this
agreeable occasion may not be an uninteresting incident
of 'Down the Road.' I never heard of any other
person who had the good fortune to travel with such
a set of scoundrels. In fact, on that memorable day,
my companions were 'the Chester Gaol Delivery.'

In or about the month of November 1834, I got
upon the 'Albion' coach, which ran from Birkenhead
to London, at Whitchurch in Shropshire. There was

no one on the box, so up I got by the side of the coachman. I did not at the moment take much notice of the passengers, but I recollect that the day was cold, and they looked a 'roughish lot.' I remember that I wondered why there was no one on the box, which was a very unusual thing, for the box is, and was, and I suppose always will be, the seat *par excellence* of all seats on a coach.

' I suppose you know what kind of a load we've got, sir,' said the coachman. ' No,' I said ; ' they look a queer lot ; what are they ? ' ' Why,' said he, 'they're all gaol birds.' ' Where are they going ? ' said I. ' Why, to Botany Bay,' said he ; 'and I wish they were there now, for they are inclined to give a little trouble, and would do if they had not got "ruffles" on ; but they're pretty safe, they are all fast to the rail ; ' meaning the rail that went across the coach behind the seat on the roof, to prevent the luggage slipping forward. They had two keepers, or turnkeys, with them, and there was no one else on the coach but these worthies, their attendants, and myself, and the coachman and guard of the coach. As it was known all along the road that Chester Gaol had been ' delivered,' and that her children were

going to pass that day on their way to the hulks, many
'birds of the same feather' were in waiting at the different places where we changed to say good-bye to their
old 'pals;' and it was with some difficulty that the
keepers could prevent their old acquaintances from
plying them with drink and giving them a parting
drop to keep their spirits up. Some of them looked
cold enough, for it was a real November day, and I
remarked they had not much in the shape of great-
coats and such little comforts. In spite of all the pre-
cautions taken, some of them had had quite enough,
and indeed too much, to drink, and they were somewhat inclined to be 'uproarious.' It was a comfort
to us that they were handcuffed and unable to do
mischief, for which they seemed quite ready. I got off
the coach at either Shifnall or Wolverhampton, I forget now which place it was, but I remember it was
beginning to be a little dusk, and we lit the lamps.
The coachman called my attention to two respectable-
looking men—I may say they appeared to be gentlemen—who were getting out of the coach, preceded by
a keeper. 'There's two of the same kind,' said he;
'they've been convicted of forgery, and are going to

be transported for life.' It was easy to see, as they got out of the coach, that they were handcuffed, for they were obliged to step out very 'daintily,' their hands being closely locked together in an 'iron embrace.' Being the greatest swells of the party, and all the places on the roof being occupied by the other ruffians, they had been allowed what was called 'to ride inside' with one of the turnkeys. I was delighted not to be going any further, and glad to see the coachman get on his box again and drive off with his precious load. More than one of them was half drunk, and they left, singing 'We're off to Botany Bay' at the top of their voices. It was, as it happened, a lucky thing for me that I got off when I did, for before reaching Walsall the horses shied at some sparks flying across the road from a blacksmith's shop, bolted, and, running against a lamp-post, upset the coach in the streets of Walsall. No one was killed ; but the coachman never got over the injuries he received, and, I heard, ultimately died of them.

During the confusion caused by this accident, and whilst another coach and coachman were being got ready to take them on, some of the convicts contrived to get files and other implements from their friends, and in a most artistic way got their handcuffs into such a form that they could get them off when they chose. They had made an agreement that at a certain signal they should set themselves free, and spring upon the keepers. This they did in a long, straight bit of road not far from Dunchurch. They overpowered the keepers, took their spare handcuffs, which they put on them, and paid the same attentions to the coachman and guard. They then cut the traces and let loose the horses, themselves making the best of their way across the fields. The greater part of them were retaken, but the two gentlemen forgers escaped.

CAN anyone be alive in the year 1874 who could 'lay 'is 'and upon 'is 'art' and swear that he had ever seen a real live 'Charlie' in his watch-box, with his horn lantern and his rattle; or had been in a real old hackney coach, before anything in the shape of a cab of any kind existed? Believe me, I have both seen the real old Charlie with his horn lantern in his watch-box, with his rattle stuck in his belt, and have 'ridden' often in a real old hackney coach, with its pair of worn-out dog horses, smelling of 'King Froust,' and sometimes, I fear, of 'subjects' taken by the 'body-snatchers' from some churchyard to the hospital for dissection, and for the transport of which a hackney coach was just the thing.

Often too as a boy, at that little-loved place called 'the Charter House,' have I and others let down our nightcaps (for all wore white nightcaps with a tassel to them in those days) to the old Charlie at the corner of Wilderness Row, to buy for us tarts, plums, apples, and other contraband eatables, which could only be procured by stealth, and by no better means than your nightcap and a string let down from the window with a sixpence in it for the Charlie's trouble.

But few in these days can call to mind a real foggy morning in London in winter under the influence of such lamplight as there was then. Gas was in its infancy, and oil lamps were still burning in most parts. Only fancy oil lamps in a thick London fog in the middle of winter! and only here and there a Charlie, who was oftener than not asleep in his watch-box, to protect the British public! 'Bobbies' were not born in those remote days.

We have chartered a hackney coach overnight, for which, being wanted very early in the morning, we have to pay an extra fare as a matter of course. We will proceed from Harley or Wimpole Street, the most fashionable streets in those days. We make the best of our way to the 'George and Blue Boar,' Holborn, from whence the 'Regent' coach starts at six o'clock. There is a thick fog; and, after groping along in nearly outer darkness for an indefinite length of time, we at length turn into the yard, and find the horses 'put to.'

Piles of luggage are being placed on the top and into the fore and hind boot of the coach. Where the luggage for 'four in and twelve out' used to go I will leave you to make out, for I never could. But go it did; and, having stowed our load away, we go out of the yard, down Holborn Hill, to the left up Cow Lane, through Smithfield, and make the best of our way to the 'Peacock' at Islington, meeting droves of bullocks, sheep, and all sorts of conveyances coming from Smithfield. But we have arrived safely, neither upsetting anyone nor being upset ourselves. At this I often wondered, for the steam from the horses, the breath from the horses, the cattle, and the sheep, added to the dimness of the lamps and the dense fog, turned everything into worse than darkness. You might as well have looked inside a stewpan for anything that could be seen. 'Darkness in fact was visible.' Everything else was invisible through the darkness of early morn and the fog.

Having achieved the 'Peacock' at Islington, a sight only to be seen there, and in those days, awaits us. A noise, I will call it a 'sonus quadrupedans,' assails your ears, as coach after coach comes up. All coaches

going anywhere north called there ; and, as they came
up the old hostler, or a man whoever he was, with a
horn lantern, called out their names as they arrived on
the scene. Up they come through the fog, but our old
friend knows them all. Now 'York Highflier,' now
' Leeds Union,' now 'York Express,' now 'Rocking-
ham,' now 'Stamford Regent,' now 'Truth and Daylight,' and others which I forget, all with their lamps
lit, and all smoking and steaming, so that you could
hardly see the horses. Off they go. One by one as
they get their vacant places filled up, the guard on
one playing 'Off she goes!' on another, 'Oh, dear,
what can the matter be;' on another, 'When from
great Londonderry ;' on another, 'The flaxen-headed
ploughboy ;' in fact, all playing different tunes almost
at the same time. The coaches rattling over the
stones, or rather pavement—for there was little or no
macadam in those days ; the horses' feet clattering
along to the sound of the merry-keyed bugles, upon
which many of the guards played remarkably well,
altogether made such a noise as could be heard nowhere except at the ' Peacock ' at Islington, at half-past
six in the morning. All this it was curious to hear

and see, though not over pleasant in a dense fog, particularly if it were very cold into the bargain, with
heavy rain or snow falling. It was a miserable look-
out for those who had to sit it out till they reached
York, or some place, perhaps, two or three hundred
miles from London. One dares hardly think of such
things happening to a friend, on an empty stomach, at
six o'clock on a winter's morning. Still, we have gone
through it; and ' here we am again,' as the clown says
in the pantomime, not very fresh, it is true, with a
good deal of the snow still clinging about the hair and
whiskers, but quite as well as can be expected under
all circumstances. On we go in the fog, the steam
rising from the horses as if one were sitting over one
of Barclay and Perkins's largest brewing coppers, till
we get about to Highgate Archway. Then morning begins to break, and the fog to clear off. On
looking round, if you are not too cold and too wet to
do so, you see London about four miles off, below
you, in such a yellow fog and smoke as no artist I
believe has attempted to paint. At Barnet, the first
change, things look a trifle better ; and, pulling up at
the inn, Tom Hennesy, of the ' Regent,' and George

Cartwright, of the 'York Express,' exchange greetings; and having had a glass of rum-and-milk, off we go again, the 'Regent' to Stamford, and the 'York Express' through Stamford to York; the 'Regent' being due at Stamford at eight the same evening, and the 'York Express' due at York about twelve hours afterwards. On a fine day in winter the journey used to be quite long enough, but in rain or snow it was almost too long; and often have I thanked my stars on arriving at Stamford, wet through, and cold to my very bones, that I had not to go on to York.

It was in one of my very early coaching days that Tom Hennesy, who was always fond of giving me a lesson in 'waggoning,' and by whose side I was sitting on the box, said, 'Now then, sir, you must take 'em a bit;' and, having changed sides with him, we went on very satisfactorily between Hatfield and Wellyn. Having arrived near to that place, where we changed horses, 'Now then,' said Tom, 'I'd better take them down the hill,' which was a pretty steep one. 'It would never do for old Barker'—who kept the 'White Hart,' at Wellyn, and horsed the coach— 'to see you driving; he's a three-cornered old beggar, and if he saw you "working" he'd kick up a d——l of a row.' The words were hardly out of his mouth, when who should appear but the 'three cornered old beggar' himself, walking up the hill. 'Blessed if there aint old Barker,' said Tom; 'that's a nice go. Never mind, it can't be helped; catch 'em fast by the head, and go down steady. Don't look as if you

H

seed him; we'll make the best we can of it.' So
down we went to the inn door, where the horses were
standing ready to change. By the time we had got
the horses out of the coach, old Barker, who had
turned round the moment we had passed him, and
who looked anything but pleasant, was down upon us.
Tom was all ready for action and was all for the first
blow. ' Good morning, Mr. Barker, sir. Did you ever
see a young gentleman take a coach steadier down
a hill ? 'Pon my word, sir, he could not have done it
better. He's a pupil of mine, sir, and I'm blessed if he
did not do it capital; don't you think he did, sir, for
you seed him ?' ' Hum,' said old Barker ; ' you know
it's all against the laws. Supposing anything happened,
what then?' ' Well, sir, I did not expect anything
would happen, with such horses as these of yours ;
there's no better four horses, sir, betwixt London and
Stamford ; and as for those wheelers, why, they'll hold
anything.' This, of course, was pouring balm into old
Barker's wounds, which seemed to heal pretty quickly,
and he put on a pleasanter face, and said, ' Well,
Hennesy, you know I don't like " gentlemen coachmen," and, above all things, very *young* ones. Don't

you do it again.' The horses being to, and our friend
Tom having hold of his reins and his foot upon the
wheel, he just observed, 'No one going to-day, sir?'
and got upon his box. As soon as we were off, 'Well,
he was wonderful civil, for *him*,' said Tom; 'but, as I
said before, he's a cross-grained, three-cornered old
beggar, at the best of times, and if I could only catch
him lying drunk in the road I'd run over his old neck
and kill him, blessed if I wouldn't. What business had
he to be walking up the hill? I suppose he thought he
should catch me "shouldering?"'

EXPLANATION OF 'SHOULDERING.'

FOR the edification of those who were never on a
coach it may be well to describe what the term
'Shouldering' means.

'Shouldering,' or carrying 'shoulder sticks,' was
this: '*Thro*' Passengers,' or any passengers getting on
to the coach at any inn, or change, where there was
an authorised booking-office, were entered in the 'way
bill,' and the proceeds thereof went into the pockets

of the proprietors of the coach. It would, however,
sometimes happen that some person would meet
the coach on the road *between* the towns, or
changes, who wanted '*a ride*' without going through
the *form* of 'booking,' and as he could probably
get off for *much less* by making friends with
the coachman than he would in the regular way,
this kind of conversation would take place between
him and the coachman who pulls up to see if he's
worth having : 'Can you give us a ride to-day ?'
'How far are you going?' 'Oh! only to Biggleswade, or Huntingdon,' or any other town he might
name. 'How much do you want?' 'Five shillings,'
perhaps the coachman would say, or whatever he
thought his passenger, to be, would be *likely* to give.
'Very well, I don't mind giving that.' 'Jump up
then, I'll pull up before we get into the town, and you
can walk through whilst we're changing, but you must
mind and not let "Old Crouch," or "Old Barker," or
whoever horsed the coach, see you ; but you must
look sharp, and get a bit out of the town whilst we
are changing. Remember—I'll pull up for you when
I catch you up on the other side of the town.' Thus,

our friend would again resume his seat, and at the
next town or change perform the same 'anticks' till he
arrived at his destination, when the coachman would
take the five shillings and what is called 'Stuff the
Monkey' with it, and thus do his little bit of
'Shouldering,' which upon some occasions was not
otherwise than a profitable trade. But it required a
little caution, as some of the 'shoulder sticks' were
occasionally not 'up to the time of day' and if
they were *suspected* of such dodges, the innkeeper
would be a bit suspicious and be on the look-out.
And if anything was found out the coachman was
severely handled for 'Shouldering.'

It's forty years since, at the very least, that, sitting by the side of Tom Hennesy on the ' Regent ' coach, bound for Stamford, we started from the ' George and Blue Boar,' Holborn. It was a lovely morning, I well remember, in summer; and as we passed on our way the smoke from the chimneys was rising in endless blue puffs, emitting every now and then a smell of pine wood, or deal, from the little white bundles of kindling so well known to all housemaids in London. The smell of an early breakfast, or of something frying and denoting such a meal, occasionally greeted one's nose as we passed along the streets, and seemed to say that the different shopkeepers and tradesmen were about to fortify their inner man against the toils of the day. We pass along down Holborn Hill, and arrive at ' the Peacock at Islington.' Stopping a few minutes to take up passengers and parcels, we start again, and, passing through Highgate Archway, arrive at our first change at Barnet. The

view from Highgate Archway on such a morning was
beautiful, and a thing to be remembered all one's life.
Looking over London from the high ground at Highgate, on a really clear day, with the smoke curling up
from the endless chimneys, and the early morning sun
shining out and lighting up all around, was perfectly
lovely. There were no great, tall, ugly chimneys in
those days pouring out their volumes of black smoke,
and making the whole town and country around look
like a mining district. Gasworks and iron foundries
were not so common in those days as they are
now, and, though there were some to be seen, they
were comparatively few and far between. As we trot
along merrily, the fresh, early morning air is most exhilarating. The labourer is plodding his way to his
work with his pipe in his mouth. What a fragrant
smell is wafted back as we pass him! The light
morning breeze brings back the odour of his morning
pipe. The mixture of shag tobacco and early morn
is too delightful, and puts to shame all other mixtures;
even Mr. Simmons's mixture at fourteen shillings a
pound would have been nowhere.

But we have come to our first change at Barnet,

and our fresh team is standing ready before the door
of the 'Green Man.' Whilst the horses are being put
into the coach, Tom and I slip into the bar and get
a glass of rum-and-milk, which the pretty barmaid has
always ready for Tom, for, though a married man, Tom
was always a great favourite with the ladies. You,
good reader, may not be aware what rum-and-milk
is, and the soothing effect it has upon an empty stomach.
The composition is simple, soothing, and at the same
time exhilarating, and stands thus : A tumbler of quite
fresh milk, one fair lump of sugar, two table-spoonfuls
of rum, and just a thought of nutmeg grated on to the
top of all.

'Now, then, sir,' says Tom, 'you shall work this
stage ; catch hold of them, and don't let the apron touch
the old mare, or she'll kick the boot in.' Away we
go ; and, just as we had got out of the town, I saw one
of the worst croppers I ever saw, or ever wish to see
again ; I only wonder that we had not to attend a
coroner's inquest. The case was this :—

An old man was driving a cart, and was sitting on
the side rail. It was rather early in the day for him
to be asleep ; but he was asleep, and I suppose his

reins had slipped out of his hand. As we passed him,
' I'll wake him up,' said Tom ; and, suiting the word to
the threat, ' Hi !' said Tom, as loud as he could halloa.
The poor old fellow pulled sharp at his reins, which
being at the bottom of his cart did not answer to his
call, and over he went backwards over the wheel a
regular somersault. I don't know why he was not
killed on the spot, but he got up and shook himself.
I conclude he thought that he had merely tumbled
out of bed. He had, however, a slight cut on his
head, which he did not seem to think of much con-
sequence. It was no fault of mine, nor indeed of any
one; but I gave him half-a-crown, and told him to go
and 'get something to drink,' which I believed was
the panacea for all things in those days, as it is in
these. The old fellow seemed highly delighted, and
I have no doubt got very drunk, particularly as, being
early in the day, he would have lots of time to do it
in, and plenty to do it *with*.

' Tom,' said I, as I threw my thong lightly under
the near side bar, and just reminded my leader that
he must do his share of the work, ' where *did* you
get this stick ? ' It was a real beauty, with a crook,

I

or, as they used to call it, a 'dog's leg,' just above the
handle, and was one of Joseph and William Ward's
make. 'Where did I get it? A friend of mine gave
it me,' said Tom ; 'and there's his name on the handle.'
On the brass ferule was the name of ' R. Bonus.' ' Just
pull up at that door,' said Tom, as we neared a public-
house on the left-hand side of the road, ' and be sure
to read the name over the door. Whatever you do,
mind and keep your hand over the dog's leg.' ' What's
up now ?' said I. ' Never you mind,' said Tom, ' but
just do as I tell you ; I'll tell you my reason when we
get off again.' As soon as we were fairly off again,
' Well,' said Tom, ' what do you think is up ? Did you
mind the name over the door, as I bid you ?' ' Yes,'
I said ; ' it's the same name as the name on the whip.'
' Well,' said he, ' that whip belonged to Bonus.' ' And
you prigged it from him, I suppose ?' I said. ' No,'
said he, ' not exactly that ; but I've got it, and I don't
mean him to have it again, if I can help it. Don't
you see,' he said, ' I used always to leave one of my
whips behind Bonus's door. Now, I cautioned Bonus
never to use it, for he was very fond of driving, and
used sometimes to drive one of the vans when he

TOM HENNESY'S CROOKED WHIP

could get a chance. Well, one day I took my whip
from behind the door, and found that it was broken.
I put it back again without his seeing me, and took
his ; and if you'll promise me that you'll take it clean
out of the country, and never bring it into these parts
again, I'll make you a present of it.' On these terms
I became the happy possessor of the dog-legged stick ;
and, though I have driven hundreds of miles with it
on other roads, it has never been a single mile on the
London side of Stamford.

'Tom,' said I one day, as this worthy gave one of his shrillest of whistles, and hit his near-side leader, as he could hit him, clean and neat under the bar— one, two, three, and a draw that made him skip up into his collar, and fairly wakened him up—'Tom,' I said, 'I think you can whistle louder, hit a horse harder, and tell a bigger lie than any man I ever knew.' 'You're right, sir; you're right,' said Tom; 'I can, I can, I believe I can, I think I can, do them all as well and as neat as here and there one. Why, bless you, sir, there's some of 'em as never *could* hit a horse ; and as for hitting a near-side leader, why they set a picking at 'em as if they were trying to pick a penny out of a pint pot, instead of turning their wrists under and letting their thong go in this way;' suiting the action to the word, and giving the aforementioned leader a repetition of the dose, and pretty nearly taking his hind leg off.

'Now, as to lying, though I don't own to being a regular liar, still there's sometimes when you must lie a bit. There's some folks that you can't get on with at all if you can't lie ; and unless you lie well there's no use in lying at all, as I can see ; and unless you can lie pretty well I should like to know who could compass Old Barker of Wellyn, or that long, sour old beggar at Biggleswade.' This was a certain Mr. Crouch, where the up coach always dined, and who kept the inn in those days ; and where on a really cold day in winter the process of dining was carried on under no small amount of difficulty. Your hands were frozen, your feet were frozen, your very mouth felt frozen, and, in fact, you felt frozen all over. Sometimes, with all this cold, you were also wet through, your hat wet through, your coat wet through, the large wrapper that was meant to keep your neck warm and dry wet through, and, in fact, you are wet through yourself to your very bones. Only twenty minutes was allowed for dinner ; and by the time you had got your hands warm enough to be able to untie your neck wrapper, and had got out of your great-coat, which, being wet, clung tenaciously to you, the time for feed-

ing was half gone. By the time you had got one
quarter of what you could have consumed had your
mouth been in eating trim, and your hands warm
enough to handle your knife and fork, the coachman
would put his head in, and say : 'Now, gentlemen, if
you please; the coach is ready.' After this summons,
having struggled into your wet great-coat, bound your
miserable wet wrapper round your miserable cold
throat, having paid your two and sixpence for the
dinner that you had the will but not the time, to eat,
with sixpence for the waiter, you wished the worthy
Mr. Crouch good day, grudged him the half-crown he
had pocketed for having dined so miserably, and again
mounted your seat, to be rained and snowed upon,
and almost frozen to death before you reached London.

'You look cold, sir,' said Tom, as he turned round and spoke to a gentleman who was flapping his hands and trying to warm himself, just as we were nearing Stevenage on the Great North Road. The Six Hills at Stevenage were generally the subject for a bet of a glass of brandy-and-water; and I suppose he thought that the gentleman in question, being in nowise over warm, would not mind having a bet for a glass of 'something hot.' 'Do you know the Six Hills at Stevenage, sir?' said Tom. 'Well, sir, do you know they are very curious; they do say that they are old tombs or places where they used to bury people, but the odd thing is that no one can tell which two of them are the furthest apart—'I'll just pull up as we pass them, sir, and I'll bet you a glass of brandy-and-water, or rum-and-water, or whatever you like so long as it's hot—for it's precious cold to-day—that you can't tell me which two of them are the furthest apart.' There was a slight difference, but not so much as to be very perceptible. 'Well, I'll bet you a glass of brandy-and-water, coachman, that those two,' pointing to two of them, 'are the furthest apart from each other.' 'Well, then, sir,' said Tom, 'you've lost your bet, and we will have a glass each at the next change, which you shall pay for. They may seem so, but the *first* and the *last* are the furthest apart, are they not, sir?' 'Why, of course they are,' said the gentleman. 'Then, sir, you owe me a glass of brandy-and-water;' which of course was duly accounted for at the next stage.

THE chances are a hundred to one that in these days
the reader never saw or heard of the 'road game,'
which was sometimes also called 'road piquette;' and
when I have informed him what it was, he may probably consider it a slow proceeding, and hardly
worth the name of an amusement to pass the time.
In these days of rapid movement, when one goes so
fast that one can hardly count the telegraph posts
or distinguish how many wires there are, the 'road
game' cannot well be played, and with newspapers
and books to read in the train it would be a slow
proceeding. But on a coach, doing nine, or even ten
miles an hour, instead of forty, time sometimes hung
rather heavily on hand, and we were glad to have
a game of any sort to beguile the hours that were
sometimes rather tedious. Though there were generally plenty of incidents along the road, still if incidents did not present themselves just when wanted,

K

the 'road game' was sometimes played; and I have
seen as much amusement and jollity over it, and I
may say excitement, as if there had been a pack
of cards and whist inside a railway carriage. The
coachman, for instance, and the person sitting beside
him, would have a game, tossing up for taking choice
of which side of the road they would have. A don-
key counted seven, a pig one, a black sheep one, a
cat five, a cat in a window ten, a dog one, a magpie
one, a grey horse five; and there was one thing by
which game . might be got at once, but it was connected with what I cannot venture to describe, and it
was a very rare occurrence. Once in my life, and
only once, I saw this feat performed, and it elicited
a shout of 'Game, by Jove!'

HOW TO 'FIX THEM.'

POOR Tom Hennesy, after having for many years driven the 'Regent' coach from Huntingdon to London every other day—up on Mondays, Wednesdays, Fridays ; down Tuesdays, Thursdays and Saturdays—was, like many others, run off the road by the rail, and 'faut de mieux' took to driving a pair-horse coach from Cambridge to Huntingdon and back. It so happened that I found myself seated by him one morning, from Cambridge to Huntingdon. 'Why, Tom,' I said, as we got a little way down the street, 'you've got a pair of real pulling brutes there; they'll run away with you as soon as you get out of the town.' 'Not they,' said Tom ; 'I'll *fix them* as soon as we get past the toll-bar ; they'll go pleasant enough then.' Accordingly, when a short way through the toll-bar, he pulled up, and with a ' Just hold them a

K 2

bit, sir, will you?' he descended, and from his pocket
he pulled out a cord. 'What have you got there?'
said I. 'Oh! I'm only going to *fix them*,' said Tom.
He began at once to perform the operation, which
consisted in putting a sort of loop into each of their
mouths, and slipping another loop over the roller
bolts. Having got up again, 'Now then,' says Tom,
'perhaps you'll like to pull the coach by your mouths;
I can tell you you shan't pull my arms off any more.
Now, will you believe it, sir,' said he, 'whenever
they gets anything that's extra bad, and as no one
else can manage, they sends them to me because
they knows as I can *fix them;* but they don't know
how I fixes them, for I always take this penny cord
off and puts it into my pocket again before I gets
to Fenny Stanton. There's no use letting every one
know how you do business.' Poor old Tom! he was
a roughish fellow, but a good fellow at heart, and
could what he called *fix them* better than any man
I ever knew; he was 'as full of dodges as a tree full
of monkeys.'

I remember once between Buckden and St. Neot's,
on the North Road, that a brown mare with a tanned

muzzle excited his wrath by jibbing and scotching and hanging back, and as she was on a good road, and there was no seeming reason for her doing so, he pitched into her ; at last he said, 'What's the matter with the mare, I wonder ? ' and having got down, he found her off thigh broken and the bone actually protruding through the skin. It is a curious fact, but I once again saw the same accident occur. I was posting with two gentlemen in an open barouche, going to a large county meeting at Sleaford in Lincolnshire ; all of a sudden the horse which the postboy had in hand, and which was a big chestnut, fell dead lame, and we came to a standstill. The postboy got off his horse and we out of the carriage, and having seen the thing before, I said at once the horse had broken his thigh, which proved to be the case. The two gentlemen who saw the accident, and who were with me in the carriage, are still alive, and can vouch for what I say, unless a lapse of forty years has rendered their memories as hazy as the ' soi-disant ' Sir Roger Tichborne's. The road in both cases was a perfectly smooth turnpike road, without loose stones or ruts. or anything to account for what

happened. I well remember that on both occasions
the day was broiling hot and the dust flying, so that
there was no extra draught from the road being bad,
nor heavy from rain or wet of any kind.

STILTON cheese cannot have much to do with coaching, you will say, but still it had. For many years the Stilton cheeses sold at Stilton were more in number than in any other place; and though not one of them was made there, they were supposed to be by those who knew no better.

Stilton was on the Great North Road, between Huntingdon and Stamford, and there were somewhere about forty-two coaches and mails passing through every twenty-four hours, not to mention the endless carriages posting north and south. As Stilton was so famed for Stilton cheeses, the sale of them was very large; and many was the passenger by the coaches or mails, or amongst those who were posting, that bought a Stilton cheese of the worthy hostess of the inn where 'the change' was, a fat, upstanding, portly dame, by name Miss Worthington. You might have thought from her appearance, as she held aloft a Stilton cheese on a tray to the passengers on the coach, saying, 'Pray, sir, would you not like a Stilton cheese to take home with you?' that the said Stiltons might have been made at home.

Mr. Chafe Justice, darlint, now, 'did ye ever see the like of that?'

As at present, so then were they made in Leicestershire, from which county they were sent to Stilton, and were sold in great numbers to those travelling on the Great North Road, which in fact was the road everywhere, and hence they got the name of 'Stilton cheeses.'

I remember one day, when on the coach with an old uncle of mine, who had lived in Leicestershire a good deal and hired a place for hunting near Melton, that the said Miss Worthington, as was her usual custom, was persecuting him to buy a Stilton cheese. She swore that Stilton cheeses were all made at Stilton, and it was with the greatest difficulty that he could persuade her that she was going fast to the d——l for telling lies and sticking to them; and she was a little taken aback when he said, 'Why Miss Worthington, you know perfectly well that no

Stilton cheese was ever made at Stilton; they're all
made in Leicestershire; and therefore, as you say
your cheeses are made at Stilton, they cannot be
good : I won't have one.' No doubt she wondered
who he was to be so knowing; everyone knew Miss
Worthington of Stilton, though she might not know
everyone that knew her, upon the same principle
that 'more know Tom Fool than Tom Fool knows.'
You will say with truth that the Stilton cheese story
has not much to do with coaching, but still, as the
little incident I have related happened on a coach, it
is an incident of the Road, and may enlighten some,
even in these days, as to *where* Stilton cheeses *do* come
from. I do verily think that a Stilton cheese in
1828 was a 'better fellow' than he is in 1874, unless
by mere chance. Hardly anyone, in the days I have
named, used to eat Stilton cheese except 'swells.' In
those days I suspect that they put less milk in their
cream and less water in their milk than they do now,
and that from this cause Stiltons were altogether a
better article. Everywhere, now-a-days, one sees Stilton cheese, and where one man used to eat it in 1828
a thousand eat it in 1874, if you can call the article

that one sees in the *shape* of a Stilton by that name, but which in reality is, generally speaking, a composition of chalk, lard, flour, and everything to resemble, if possible, the article it *ought* to be made of, which is simply *cream*. The real, rich, genuine, old Stilton that used to be on the table at dinner, or rather at 'cheese time,' and was helped by the master of the house with a silver cheese scoop with an ivory handle to it, and the long glass of ale, or the glass of 'old brown crusted port,' which was handed round by the important-looking old butler with his jolly red nose and white waistcoat, is, like the coaches and mails and coachmen and guards, gone. 'Dinner à la Russe' having become the fashion, Stilton cheese and the glass of good old port are almost things unknown. So much for Stilton cheese and Miss Worthington.

I had almost forgotten the little anecdote of the good Miss Worthington which follows; and though it has no more to do with actual coaching than Stilton cheese, it may amuse. Two old lady relations of mine, chancing to stop a night at the hotel in Stilton, on their way from London to Stamford, feeling a little 'rheumaticky' in the morning, as many old ladies are apt to do, made up their minds that they had had a *damp bed*. They forthwith summoned the worthy hostess into their presence as they sat at breakfast, and hinted to her that their bed must have been damp, not know-ing how in any other way to account for their sensa-tions. Miss Worthington was horror-struck, and was full of indignation at such a thing being thought pos-sible. The ladies stuck to it that such *must* be the case, and that the rheumatic feeling must be caused by the bed being *damp*. 'Indeed, ma'am,' said Miss Worthington, 'I never heard of such a thing as a damp bed in *my house*, and I am sure, ma'am, I never was accused of such a thing before.' 'Well,' said one of the ladies, 'I assure you that both my sister and I thought it felt damp when we went to bed, but we did not like to say anything at the time.' 'Well, ma'am,' said Miss Worthington, 'all I can say is, I never heard of a damp bed in Stilton before, and if it was so it must have been from the perspiration of the two people who slept in it the night before last. I cannot account for it in any other way.'

WITHIN a few miles of Stilton, and between Stilton
and Stamford, is a hill called Alconbury Hill. In the
days I am writing of, so famous for Miss Worthington
and her Stilton cheeses (about the year 1824, and
from before that time to 1828 or 1829), there used to
be in that part of the country an incredible number of
kites—the 'Forked-tail Kyte,' '*Falcon Milvus*' Lin.
'Le Milan Royal' Buff, or what in Scotland were called
'Gleads,' the red feathers of whose forked tail were
famous for wings of salmon-flies. These birds used
to be soaring over the road, and over a wood called
Moncks Wood—a wood famed in the Fitzwilliam
country; in almost every direction one used actually
to see them sitting in the middle of the road, and on
one occasion I remember counting as many as twenty-
seven in the air at the same time. The preservation
of game, I suppose, has got rid of them, for no such
bird is to be seen now; and it is wonderful to think

how in a few years those birds have become almost
extinct throughout England. I have not seen one for
at least thirty years, common as they used to be in
the days of Stilton cheeses, Miss Worthington, and
the old ' Stamford Regent Coach.'

'WHAT, DRUNK AGAIN, YOU LAZY OLD BEGGAR.'

IT was during my college days that the following took place. It was on a fine summer's morning, or rather I should say, 'in the merry, merry month of May,' that when travelling by the 'Louth Mail,' and coming in sight of our change, our 'Jehu' turning round on his box, accosted the guard with, ' Now, Jemmy, blow your horn : I don't see any horses out.' Jemmy at once responded to the call, and 'gav' em a couple of blasts' on the 'sweet-toned instrument.' 'Whatever can be up ?' said Jemmy, as he again put the horn to his mouth and gave a still louder and more *impressive* blast, which also seemed to have no effect. 'Oh! I see how it is,' said he. ' Drunk again last night I'll warrant;' and with this we arrived at a little wayside kind of stables, or barn-looking edifice standing all alone by the side of the road. A step-ladder stood against a door in the side of the building and pro-

claimed that it led to the hay-loft. No horses were to
be seen, and nothing seemed to be alive at such an
early time of day except a cock and hen, who were
evidently on the look-out for their morning meal.
'Brave chanticleer' was proclaiming the morn, to the
best of his ability, and seemed almost to be standing
on tiptoes to effect his purpose. Still nothing else
showed any signs of life. Jehu got down and began to take out his horses himself, with a 'D— that
drunken old rascal! I'll bet he's asleep in the hay-loft;
just nip up, Jemmy, and pull him down neck and crop,
if you can find him.' Whereupon Jemmy sprung up
the ladder, found his man fast asleep, and seizing him
by the legs, pulled him down 'bodily' into the road,
exclaiming, 'What, drunk again last night, were you,
you lazy old beggar! Who do you think is going to do
your work for you, I wonder?' Accidents will happen
in the best regulated families, they say, and this was
one of them 'on the Road,' and it was a somewhat
unusual one to happen to a mail.

I GO TO LIVE NEAR THE HOLYHEAD ROAD.

Such are some remembrances of my younger days,
I may say, my 'beardless youth.' As time went on
my mode of life changed, and being married I went
to live in Shropshire, within a couple of miles of the
great Holyhead Road, and between Shrewsbury and
Oswestry. I there became acquainted with my old
and much esteemed friend, the Honourable Thomas
Kenyon, who lived hard by, and who was a well-
known good whip. We fraternised a good deal; and
if I wanted a character from any coach proprietor he
would always give me one, 'for honesty, sobriety, and
steadiness,' in proof of which he on more than one
occasion trusted me to drive his coach, which was the
greatest compliment he could pay any one. He used
to drive from his own house to Shrewsbury, from
which he lived thirteen miles, every day but Friday,
and he kept two teams of short-legged chestnuts to
work his coach. I had now got into a part of the

world where the coaches were fast, and where some
of them 'ran in opposition.' The Holyhead Mail was
very fast, and the 'Oak' and 'Nettle' coaches from
Welchpool to Liverpool ran in opposition, and were
often too fast to be quite safe, as I sometimes used to
fancy. However, whatever was the pace required, I
had to do it when I drove, which I did pretty often.
Both ran within half a mile of my door when I lived
between Oswestry and Llanymyneck ; and, as I had
friends living both at Wrexham and Chester, I often
used to drive the coach so far. I knew the coachmen on both coaches, but I used generally to drive
the ' Nettle.' I remember one day, when I got on the
' Nettle,' Shaw Evans, who was one of the coachmen,
said to me, as I got on the coach at Wrexham, ' Have
you heard of poor Jack Mathews, sir ? ' to which I
replied, ' No,' not at all guessing what was the matter.
It seems that Jack Mathews, who drove the ' Oak,'
took it into his head to go for a day's outing to
Liverpool. He got on the railway, which was hardly
finished, somewhere near Wrexham, intending to go
as far as Chester. From some mishap the bridge at
Chester was insecure, and only a temporary one ; it

broke down, and poor Jack Mathews and another man were killed dead on the spot. A friend of mine and his son, Mr. W. Wynne, were precipitated in the railway carriage into the river Dee. How they were got out I forget; but as I have seen my friend W. Wynne since, I know he was not killed. Poor Jack Mathews would have been safer driving the 'Oak' coach, in all probability, for he was as pretty a coachman as ever had four horses in hand, and was altogether a good workman in all respects; always as 'smart as a new pin.'

THERE was no better mode of travelling in my day
than by the Holyhead Mail, which passed through
Shrewsbury; and as I lived for some time close to
the Holyhead road between Shrewsbury and Oswestry, and as I was often travelling by it, and had leave
from all the proprietors from Shrewsbury to Holyhead
to drive their horses, I had a good opportunity of
knowing everything about it. It was, perhaps, as fast
a mail as any going, except perhaps the Davenport
or Quicksilver mail, being rated by the Post Office at
rather more than ten miles and a half an hour, including stoppages. I always considered that we did
eleven miles an hour, including stoppages; but, be that
as it may, it was a very fast mail. It was well horsed,
of course, as a general rule; but there were, of course,
some 'sticky ones' during the journey. I did not
know much of this mail on the London side of Shrews-

bury; but from Shrewsbury to Holyhead I knew every coachman and guard, the horses, horsekeepers, and I might almost say every stone on the road. The road, however, was so good, that unless you went to a stone-heap, I don't think you could have found a stone big enough to pelt a robin with; added to this, it was so beautifully planned that there was not a hill in the whole distance from Shrewsbury to Holyhead that you could not trot up and down, and, as far as my memory serves me, we never had to put on the skid during the whole of the 107 miles from Shrewsbury to Holyhead. The road when it got into Wales ran through some very hilly country, but thanks to the immortal Telford he had overcome all difficulties, and the road throughout was pretty nearly as smooth as one of Mr. Thurston's best billiard tables. I had leave from all the proprietors to drive their teams, either in the Holyhead Mail, or in any other coach horsed by them. Thus I was not putting myself under an obligation to any of the coachmen for allowing me to drive by stealth, and everything was straightforward and above-board in this respect. Whenever I appeared, the thing was a matter of course, and I was coachman for the day. As the expression was, I 'worked the coach.' The road was good, the horses were good, as a rule, the coachmen and guards were good fellows, the pace was good. At that time of day I was young, and my health was good, and what more could a man want? There was no sitting with your reins in two hands, and your whip stuck up in a socket by your side, looking for all the world like a hazel stick with a woodbine growing round it; or laid on the roof of the coach, or perhaps held by a friend who is sitting behind you, or by some one on the box beside you. Such things I have actually seen, but not on the mail. Your whip in those days was in one hand, and your reins in the other; and if you could not use them both, one for your fiddle-strings and the other for your fiddle-stick, you were of no use. If you had a sluggish team (the horses, as I said before, were as a rule good, but sometimes a new wheeler would prove to be 'a bit sticky'), and could not use your whip pretty well, and lift him off the ground and set him down half a mile on the road, as the saying was, you were of little use; for the pace was good, and as we had to keep eleven miles an hour, including stoppages,

the slugs must be made by some means to do the
pace with the others.   Eleven miles an hour, including
stoppages, stands for galloping at least the greater
part of the way.   The theory of eleven miles an hour
and the practice are two different matters.   I have
done fourteen or fifteen miles in the hour; but to keep
up eleven miles an hour for eighty or ninety miles is
a somewhat serious affair, unless your cattle are very
good.

MR. BICKNELL AND HIS HORSES.

Where is Jack Williams?

READER, do you know the London and Holyhead Road? If you are old enough to have travelled by that capital conveyance, the Holyhead Mail, you must surely remember passing near to Capel Curig, the famous 'Ogwyn Pool,' or *lake*, as we should say in England. It is a pretty spot in summer, and when the fishing season has commenced; but in the winter months it is quite the reverse, and with snow on the hills, snow falling, and a cold wind blowing from the north, I know no place much colder or more dreary and desolate, with the pool looking so cold and deep and blue that you would imagine there could be no bottom to it, the rocks above it looking so grey and cheerless, and the mountains, all covered with snow, looking like overgrown wedding-cakes. As you leave

the pool to the right going towards Holyhead, you
suddenly turn the corner, the wind blowing hard from
the north, the snow driving straight up the road
through the valley of the Ogwyn, not coming down
straight, but drifting up the road, and almost horizon-
tally with the road. Woe to the hat of the luckless
passenger who does not hold it on as he rounds that
corner! You may ask him 'Who's your hatter?' but
he will never read the name in the crown again, when
he looks into it in church on Sunday, for it is making
the best of its way into the valley beneath, having
surmounted the wall on the left hand, or with the
sudden gust is blown off to the right hand, and is
floating on the blue waters of the deep and chilly
Ogwyn. It was on such a day that I was driving
Her Majesty's Mail, when on nearing Bangor, where
we used to change horses at Bicknell's, of the Penryn
Arms, I was accosted by Charlie Harper with, 'I
think I'd better take them into Bangor, sir, for Mr.
Bicknell has given strict orders that no gentleman
should drive; there's been a row with the Post Office
because Mr. B— E— ran the mail against a waggon in Corwyn, and the mail was damaged and

delayed, and was late for the packet at Holyhead.
It so happened that a gentleman did perform this
feat, having taken a good deal of some good and
strong drink at a friend's house on the road before he
got upon the mail. At the best of times he was not
much of a coachman, but on the present occasion his
Jehuship completely forsook him, and he ran the mail
against a heavily-loaded waggon standing in the open
street at Corwyn, in the open day, without, as I have
heard, the least reason for so doing, except that he
had got too much, and could not see straight, thereby
damaging the mail, frightening the passengers, putting
the bodies of more than one of Her Majesty's liege
subjects in jeopardy, and causing so much delay that
the letters and passengers were late for the boat to
Dublin. Thus the fact of the mail being detained
through the inebriated movements of Mr. B— E—
was reported to the General Post Office, and hence
an edict was issued that in future no gentleman
should be allowed to drive. This being the case, I
most willingly gave up the reins to the authorised
Jehu, Charlie Harper. I had driven over sixty miles
in wet and wind and snow, and, to tell the honest

truth, I was pretty much tired. On arriving at the change at Bangor, I nevertheless expressed my senti- ments to Mr. Bicknell, and endeavoured to make it appear to him that it was hard to give *me* ' the sack ' for what was the fault of another. Mr. Bicknell re- gretted that so it was, and so it must be, said it was an unfortunate affair altogether, but gave me to under- stand that the law of the Post Office was like the law of certain Medes and Persians, which altered not.

Where is Jack Williams?

SOME time after the preceding anecdote headed ' Ogwyn Pool,' I got on the mail at Oswestry to go to see a friend in Anglesey. The journey, though not other- wise than prosperous, was far from pleasant, being, as usual in that latitude, wet and windy, with sleet and snow and every abomination of foul weather that could blow out of a Welsh sky in the month of De- cember. I never shall forget the wind and sleet and snow on turning the aforesaid corner of Ogwyn Pool, as we were doing our eleven miles an hour ; such a day of wind and water I scarcely ever remember ; it was hardly possible to look from under the brim of one's hat. 'Come, Charlie,' said I, as we got near Bangor, 'catch hold of them; this is Bicknell's stage, and, as he has issued his orders, I'll not drive his horses and get *you* into a scrape, which might be the case if anything went wrong.' Whereupon Charlie Harper took the mail into Bangor. Having no parcels to leave or anything to attend to, and being wet and cold and miserable, off he gets, says a word or two to one of the horsekeepers, and makes himself scarce by starting off home, never dreaming that he could be wanted any more that day. Hodgson, the guard, as soon as the mail stopped at Bicknell's door, had taken his letter-bags over his shoulder to the Post Office, some little way down the street, and soon appeared again at the corner of the street where the Post Office was, with the Holyhead and Dublin bags slung across his shoulder. But the mail that should take him and his letter-bags up at the corner of the street does not start. The horses are to and all is ready, but there is no coachman; something must be the matter. 'Where is "Chack Williams"?' cries one of the horsekeepers. 'Has anyone seen

"Chack Williams"?' says another. No one has seen
'Chack Williams;' where can he be? There stands
Hodgson at the corner of the street with his letter-
bags. Still the mail don't start; he evidently begins
to be impatient, and, seeing no one on the box, begins
to see something is wrong; at last he calls out:
'Come on; what on earth are you waiting for?'
Seeing still no signs of Her Majesty's Mail making
any kind of movement, and no appearance of any
coachman, up he comes to the mail, and in a more
energetic tone cries out: 'What the devil are you
waiting for? Where is Jack Williams?' No one had
seen Jack Williams, and no one seemed to know
whether he was dead or alive. At last one of the
horsekeepers seemed to remember all of a sudden
that Jack Williams had been summoned to attend a
magistrates' meeting on the other side of the Menai
Bridge, and that Harper was to take the mail over
the bridge, and he (Jack Williams) was to get up at
the public-house where the worthy beaks who had
summoned him were to hold their conclave. 'Yes,
indeed, I remember now; it was summoned to attend
the magistrates' meeting;' *it* standing of course for

'Chack Williams.' 'Now then,' said Hodgson, who was growing impatient; 'we can't wait here all day; somebody must drive. Mr. Reynardson, will you be so good? We shall be late for the packet.' 'I don't care,' said I, 'whether you are late or not; I am thankful to say I am not going to cross such a day as this. Jump up and drive yourself, and I'll sit behind and take charge of your bags, and play you a tune on your "grunting stick" whilst you're going over the bridge. Bicknell has said that I am not to drive his horses, and if you take root here I don't care; I'll not touch them.' 'Well, sir, we shall be late for the packet if you *won't*,' said Hodgson. 'I don't care,' said I; 'I daresay I shall be able to get to where I am going in time for dinner, or at all events before bed-time, so I'll have nothing to do with either the mail or Mr. Bicknell's horses, and if the mail, stays here all night it's nothing to me.' 'Now, Hodgson,' says Mr. Bicknell, who just then appeared at the door, 'what's the mail standing there for?' 'That's *just* what I should like to know,' answered Hodgson; 'but the mail can't go, sir, without some one to drive it. Jack Williams is not to be found, Charlie Harper has gone home long ago, and Mr. Reynardson says, you said he was not to drive your horses any more, and he won't have anything to do with them; so what's to be done I don't know. We shall be late for the packet, and then you know there'll be a row again with the Post Office people.' Things seemed to be in something of a fix, and Hodgson, though in a fuss to be off, I could see, was rather enjoying the joke, which began to be a serious one; for there seemed to be no chance of anyone to drive. It was blowing great guns, and the Menai Bridge would be rocking about like a cradle, and the team of greys, which I had often driven before, were not the handiest in the world if they had not got up the right way in the morning, and if things went a little wrong. 'Well,' said Bicknell, 'this won't do. Will you drive them, Mr. Reynardson, till you find Jack Williams on the other side of the bridge?' 'No,' said I; 'you may drive them yourself, if you like; I won't touch them.' Things looked worse and worse, as far as a start was concerned. Bicknell was no coachman himself; Hodgson said he could not drive them; I said I would not drive them; and

there seemed no one of the horsekeepers competent
to perform this feat. So, at last, Mr. Bicknell, putting
on his most affable face, said : 'Mr. R——, sir, will
you be so kind as to take them across the bridge?
I shall be very much obliged to you if you will.'
'Oh! oh!' said I, 'if you are going to be obliged,
or anything of that kind, I don't mind obliging you,
Mr. Bicknell.'

It was altogether one of the best scenes I ever
saw, and many a time after did we have our little
joke at Mr. Bicknell's expense. Well, as soon as
Mr. Bicknell had made his wishes known, I took
the mail across the Menai Bridge and picked up
'Chack Williams,' who had finished his justicing, and
was beginning to wonder what had become of the
mail. I drove Mr. Bicknell's horses to the half-way
house, where my change was, and I got down and
went to my friend's house, where I did arrive in time
for dinner. Mr. Bicknell never after said anything to
me about not driving his horses. No one horsed the
mail better than Mr. Bicknell, and his 'spicy team
of greys' were not to be surpassed by any on the
road.

MEETING OF TWO OLD ETONIANS.

On my return home into Shropshire from my friend's house in Anglesey, a rather amusing occurrence took place. On going through Bangor, though we changed horses in the town, we always pulled up at Mr. Bicknell's hotel, the 'Penryn Arms,' for a moment, to see if there were any passengers going. 'There's a gentleman to take up at the "Penryn Arms,"' said the bookkeeper, as we were starting from the house where we changed horses in the town. A couple of blasts from Hodgson's horn gives notice as we near the hotel that the mail is at hand. 'Now then,' cries Hodgson, as we pull up, and the waiter appears with his white napkin under his arm, 'is the gentleman ready? Look sharp; we're rather behind time; we can't wait.' 'Stop a pit—stop a pit!' says the Welsh waiter. 'It's coming in a moment; it's just done its breakfast; it's coming directly; it's a nice gentleman, Mr. Hodgson.

I know you can wait one minute, if you choose.' In
less than half a minute out came some of his luggage,
and amongst other things a shako case was put into
the front boot. 'Oh! oh! soger officer,' said I ; 'let
me look at his name,' which was on a brass plate.
'Major Stock, —— Regiment.' I knew the name at
once, and it entered my head that it might be an old
schoolfellow ; and I said to myself, I wonder whether
it can be the Stock I knew at Eton. Upon his coming
out and getting up to take his place beside me on
the box, what should I see but the old familiar face
that had been almost next to me at Eton for more
than four years. There never was such a country for
foul weather in winter time, I verily believe, as the
country around Bangor ; and, as on former occasions,
it was raining, and blowing, and hailing, and snow-
ing, and the elements seemed to be vying with each
other which could be the most disagreeable ; it was
as horrible a day as could be, as was the usual state
of things in those latitudes. I was in a thick weather-
proof old macintosh, such as coachmen used to wear
in those days, and had on a queerish-looking water-
proof hat, and looked, I conclude, more like a regular

son of Jehu than a gentleman who had been educated
at that 'seat of religious education and sound learning' where we had both been for so long together.
He did not seem to recognise his old schoolfellow in
the least ; and as he made himself as snug and water-
tight as circumstances would admit of, he said, 'Well
coachman, this *is* a beastly day ; we shall have a foulish
time of it, I suspect.' 'Yes, sir,' I said ; 'I'm afraid
you'll get very wet. Would you not like to go inside ?
No one would choose to go outside such a day as this
unless they were obliged ; you'd better get inside.
You'll be very wet and uncomfortable before you get
to London, if you're going so far, and it goes on like
this.' My friend, however, did not choose to go inside,
and away we went through the sleet, and wind, and
rain, chatting away, and as merry as crickets. The
pace was good, for we kept eleven miles an hour,
and he said he had never travelled on a better mail,
or had been out on a much more abominable day ; but
nevertheless, in spite of the weather, he was very sorry
that he could not go all the way to India by so good
a conveyance, and was most chatty and agreeable. I
own I could hardly keep my countenance at times, and

sometimes thought that I should fairly break down,
and that he would find me out. I did, however,
manage to do it till I had had some fun out of him.
Something turned the conversation to other roads and
other coaches, and in time we got to talk of *Windsor*
and *Eton;* and he informed me of the impositions that
were practised on a certain coach that ran from London to Eton, and driven by one of the proprietors,
Bill Moody, the firm being Thumwood and Moody,
who, I well remember, used to stop at a public-house
not far from Slough, and draw the unfortunate boys
going back to Eton for 'Coachman, please sir,' and
any extortionate charge he could make for pretended
extra luggage. He informed me of many little matters of the same kind relating to his Eton days. 'I
suppose, sir,' said I, 'that you were at Eton College,'
hardly able to keep my countenance. 'Oh, yes; I
was there four or five years,' said he; 'and a jolly
place it was, taking it as a school, though for my own
part I never could quite make out why school days
were thought so happy, and called "happy school
days."' 'Well, sir,' said I. looking him as full in the
face as the sleet, and wind, and rain, and snow, would

permit me to do, 'since you were at Eton, perhaps
you can tell me how it used to go. Was it not some-
thing in this way : Lord Lincoln, Spottiswoode Major,
Colville Minor, Reynardson Major, Stock, Boteler,
Bromhead, Bowle, Tickell, Vyse Major, and so forth ?'
'Good gracious,' said he, all amazement, 'were you at
Eton ?' 'Yes, sir,' I said ; 'I was.' 'Why,' said he,
looking hard at me, 'it surely must be Reynardson
Major.' 'Yes, sir,' I said ; 'it is the *very man.*' 'Good
heavens, old fellow !' he said, holding out his hand ;
'I did not know you in that hat and macintosh, and
driving the mail ; but I am very glad to meet you
again. Do tell me, how the deuce did you come to
this ?' Well, this was 'a facer ;' but I kept my countenance. 'How did I come to this ? Why, you see,'
said I, 'we all have our ups and downs in life, I suppose, and I have had mine. I have been a bit wildish ;
and what with a little betting, a little racing, and a
little fastish living, I've got a bit down in the world,
do you see, and so I thought it would be better to
get an honest livelihood than to steal or do anything
worse ; and as I was always fond of a bit of driving,
I have taken to this.' 'Well, old fellow,' said he, 'I

am glad at any time to meet an old schoolfellow ; but
I am sorry to hear all you have been telling me.'

Well, we went on talking over old times for a
long while. At last I could keep my own counsel no
longer, and let out to him the real state of things,
and that I was only an 'amateur.' I felt sorry afterwards that I had not more presence of mind, for to a
certainty I should have drawn him for a sovereign, or
something in gold. I got off the mail at Oswestry,
near which place I then lived, and he went on his
way *via* London to India, where he may be yet for
aught I know ; or he may have laid his bones in that
far-off land, for I have never seen or heard of him
since. The whip that I drove with that day hangs in
front of me, with about twenty others. '*Pristinæ
virtutis memores.*'

IT was on a piercing cold morning, about 8 A.M., as
they say in those days, that I arrived at the Cross
Keys Inn in Oswestry, in the month of January. A
real old-fashioned black frost had made the ground as
hard as frost could make it; every little puddle and
every little rut, as I drove from a friend's house where
I had been spending a couple of days, sparkled and
crackled like driving over glass, as the wheels of my
dog-cart passed over them. The good cheer that I
had been enjoying for the last two nights at my
kind old friend's had warmed my blood, and I cared
not a jot for frost, or snow, or wind, or rain. The
port wine, which used to be of the best, the claret,
which was in no way inferior, and the champagne,
which was 'première qualité supérieure,' to say nothing
of sundry and manifold glasses of old brown sherry,
real 'old brown glutinous,' that 'moved aright in the
glass:' not that mixture of quassia, or camomile flowers,

&c., that goes by the name of Amontillado, Vino de
Pasta, or some such mixture which in reality stands
for 'cough mixture,' and goes under the name of 'pale
sherry;' all these had the superiority over the frost,
and cold, and snow, or rain, or wind, or whatever
inclement weather chanced to come, and bade defiance
to them all. A light heart and a warm overcoat left
me nothing to wish for as I drove up to the door
of the Cross Keys, where the good landlady, Mrs.
Lloyd, of that then well known inn, had always a
glass of rum-and-milk ready for the coachman and
guard, who are even now arriving from Shrewsbury.

'Well, Dick,' said I, addressing the coachman,
whose name was Dick Vickers, 'what have you got
here?' as the team was being put to, for I saw that
they were fresh to me. 'Why, what I have got
here, sir, I expect you'll find out if you're going "to
work" this morning; there's four horses, but they've
only got two eyes amongst 'em, and it would be
quite as well if that horse had not any, so far as I
know, for he makes shocking bad use of them, at
times, I can tell you, and it's a good job it's daylight,
for I'm blessed if any man could keep his time with

them at night, at the pace we're obliged to go.' This
was eleven miles an hour, including stoppages. 'Well,
Dick,' said I, 'I'd rather not have anything to do
with such brutes; I shall be upsetting "Her Majesty's
paper-cart," or some such thing, and if it is to be
done you had better do it than I, I think.' 'Oh no!
get hold of them, sir,' says Dick; 'you'll fix 'em if
you can but get them through the toll-bar.' This bar
was three or four hundred yards from the inn, and
rather round a corner. This is a nice lot of brutes,
thought I to myself as I took hold of the reins and
was getting on the box. 'You must mind what
you're at with them,' says Hodgson, the guard,
who at that moment made his appearance with his
letter-bags thrown over his shoulder; 'they aren't
fit for any stranger to drive, I can tell you.' With
this pleasant bit of information up he gets to his seat
behind, in go the letter-bags into the boot, 'right'
cries Hodgson, and off we go, if going from one side
of the street to the other could be called going. I
soon found that, in addition to having only two eyes
amongst them, they had only one mouth, and that
was a one-sided one belonging to the off wheeler.

who was what was called 'swivel-headed,' and when
you pulled at him his head seemed to turn on a
pivot. Such a set of devils I never had hold of
before; they ran me on to the curbstone twice or
three times before I got out of Oswestry; and fortu-
nately, partly by main strength and a good deal of
good luck, I pulled them up all of a heap, just as
we were on to a heap of stones about fifty or sixty
yards from the toll-bar, on to which, had we run, I
verily believe I should have upset 'the apple-cart.'
'Well, aren't they rum 'uns?' said Dick, who
was sitting behind me, and rather enjoying the
fun, instead of being in what is called 'a jolly funk.'
The gentleman who was beside me on the box did
not seem to see things in the same light, as he
told me afterwards. 'I telled you they weren't fit
for no stranger to drive,' said Hodgson, laughing.
'Catch hold of them, Dick,' said I, 'for I can't drive
them, and I don't believe that you will get them
through the toll-bar without carrying away one of the
posts, and perhaps turning the barrow over.' He did,
however, clear everything, and did not carry away
the gate-post, as I feared he would do. Away we

went down the Holyhead Road, too fast to be quite pleasant, considering the kind of team. The road was as hard as iron with the frost, and as smooth as if it had been made by Thurston, of billiard table renown, instead of by Telford. The 'three blind 'uns and the bolter' were getting warmed up with their exertions, and began to pull; the mail was light, for it was Monday morning, and there were no London letters, and it rattled and bounded after them like a 'bounding brick of Babylon.' Little Dick began to look as if they pulled rather too hard to be pleasant, and I began to think that either the reins would go, or that he would be pulled off the box. He was, however, an uncommonly strong little chap on the box. All of a sudden, on coming to a long descent in the road—it could hardly be called a hill—what should appear right a-head of us but a long string of donkeys carrying panniers of coals on the near side of the road, and on the other a gentleman's carriage, a yellow one I remember it was, and four horses, pulled up not quite as near the side of the road as it might have been for safety, and the post-boy was down doing something to his off-side leader's harness.

'Now's your time, Dick,' said I; 'you must be
amongst some of them; keep clear of the carriage if
you can; hang the donkeys.' I could see little Dick
setting his teeth together, for they were pulling very
hard. Well, as good luck would have it, we cleared
them, except just touching the pannier on one of the
donkeys, which sent Balaam reeling against the stone
wall by the road side, and against which the lucky
animal righted again, instead of being turned over
with a hundredweight of coals or more on him. We
then proceeded safely down the long incline and up
Chirk Hill, to the 'Hand Inn,' in Chirk, where we
changed. Having our fresh team in, I again took
the helm, and we got safely to Llangollen, where
Harry Vyse (a son of the then well-known Mr. Vyse
of Wolverhampton, who horsed the mail and many
other coaches) was driving for Morris, who was ill,
and waiting for the mail coming from Holyhead. 'I
say, Harry,' said Dick, 'you'll have a pretty job with
those horses from Chirk, if you don't mind what you're
up to; we've had a nice job with them this morning,
and have almost run into a gentleman's carriage and
killed a lot of donkeys. They're a real rum lot, and

you must mind what you're at with them.' 'Oh!'
said Harry Vyse, 'I'll mind them; I can "fix them,"
I'll be bound.' Nevertheless, as Dick Vickers told
me afterwards, he had a real job with them, and,
what with one mishap or another, lost nearly half
an hour between Chirk and Oswestry. It is curious,
but certainly fully twenty years after the incident I
have related, I was telling the story to my son, who
was with me in an open conveyance with four wheels,
going to fish at Bala, and on asking the driver if he
had been long in the country, he said he had been a
post-boy, and he remembered what I have related well,
for he was the post-boy who was down altering the
leader's harness at the time when Dick Vickers was
so nearly aboard of the gentleman's yellow carriage
and the donkeys.

'DICK,' said I, addressing Dick Vickers, who was one of the coachmen on the London and Holyhead Mail, as I cast my eye round my team, at a pot-house called the 'Rising Sun,' between Llangollen and Corwen, where we changed horses, just to see that all was right, 'What's the matter with little Robin?' Robin ran off-side leader, and when I patted him, as I went round, he looked as wild as a hawk. 'Oh!' said Dick, 'Mr. Wynne, of Garthmylog, was driving yesterday, and Robin shied at a tinker with one of those wheeled grinding-stones, and he hit him, and I'll be bound he won't forget it for a week.' Robin, however, had no spite against me, and went pleasantly enough. The team consisted of four little brown cats of horses—I might almost say ponies—and were, without any ex ception, the best team I ever sat behind. They did their work more willingly and more evenly than any team I ever saw. It was always a pleasure to drive them; but they would stand no nonsense, and if once put out they could be awkward enough. The distance from the 'Rising Sun' to Corwen was six miles, and the time allowed was twenty-six minutes, in which time they did it with the greatest ease, and merrily as crickets. They could all but fly. If any one of my readers has a team that will do the six miles in the time—I mean without a touch of the whip—he has a good team. Let him take out his watch, and try what the pace is like. How few there are that are judges of pace! but this is a matter or knowledge that is very useful on a fast coach; and indeed I may say a '*sine quâ non*' on any coach, whether fast or slow.

I remember, now some years since, going down to Greenwich with the F. H. D. C., of which I am still a humble member. I had four real hard-mouthed, pulling old horses, who all wished to go first, which is a great nuisance. The coach that was in front of me was spick and span, as was the coachman, and the team was a beautiful one, 'heads and tails up,' and their knees almost hitting their mouths, their action was so fine and gaudy. After dinner, at Greenwich, and when, like Jonah of old, we were feeling ' pretty full of fish,' the subject of pace came up; and upon my saying, ' Well, I wish you'd go down a little faster, for my old horses nearly pulled my arms off,' the owner of the coach, who was in front of me, bristling up a little, said, ' Well, I think we came a very good pace. We came at least thirteen miles an hour.' ' Thirteen miles an hour!' I said ; ' why, do you know what thirteen miles an hour is ? Those old screws of mine can't do anything like thirteen miles, and it was all I could do to keep them out of your hind boot.' This was a mortal blow to the owner of the high steppers, and I don't think he ever quite forgave me ; but depend upon it, four horses with such gaudy action are not the kind to slip along, and thirteen miles an hour takes some doing with anything on wheels ; and I do not know that I ever saw a team that could do the thirteen miles within the hour without ' breaking.'

BUT I must return to the road. I was on my way to Ireland to fish, and was, as usual, driving the Holyhead Mail; old Jack Williams, the coachman, who drove daily from Holyhead to Bangor and back, was sitting beside me. A gentleman who was sitting behind tapped him on the shoulder, and this conversation took place: 'Coachman, do you know Holyhead well?' 'Me know Holyhead?' said Jack, who spoke with a strong Welsh accent. 'Yes, inteed; I suppose I to; at laste I should to; I've lived there all my life. Yes, inteed; I was pred and porn there.' 'Then you can tell me, I dare say, what is the best inn there; for I want to stay a day or two at Holyhead.' 'How should I know the best inn?' said Jack. 'Well, if you know Holyhead so well, surely you must know which is the best inn.' 'Well, inteed, I know that there's two inns in Holyhead, but I canna say which it the pest; I never goes to either of 'em.' 'Well,

but you must know which of them is called the best,
and which would be the best for a gentleman to stay
at.' 'Well, inteed,' said Jack, at last, 'I'll tell you
how it is. Should you wish to get drunk, go to
Spencer's. Should you wish to get lousy, go to
Moland's.' Spencer's was a good inn, for I have had
many a good mutton chop, and so forth, on landing
from the steamer. What Moland's was I cannot say ;
but I question whether Mr. or Mrs. Moland, or whoever kept the said inn, would feel very much flattered
by Jack Williams' account of what a person going
there was to expect.

'PLEASE will you tell me what's this writing?' said Jack Jones, as we were coming near to the lodge gates of Pentre Voilas. This was a gentleman's house on the Holyhead Road, between Cernioge and Capel Curig. 'What's this writing, Jack?' said I. 'Why, can't you read it as well as I can? it's plain enough.' 'Yes, inteed, it's plain enough,' said Jack; 'but I canna read it; it's English, and I canna read English.' 'Then why don't you get Hodgson to read it?' I said. 'Well, inteed,' said Jack, 'Hodgson willna read my parcels now. Hodgson and I are not very good friends, and he willna read my parcels; and inteed I canna get on at all sometimes.' It seems that Hodgson and Jack had had a quarrel, or 'some words,' and that Hodgson had blown Jack up for keeping bad time, at which Jack took offence and blew up Hodgson, which ended in Hodgson's refusing to read his parcels, which was mighty inconvenient to Jack, who was no great scholar in his own Welsh language, and was quite at a loss in English. It might be naturally supposed that part of the guard's duty was to read and attend to the parcels. It was so on a coach, but on a mail it was not; and though the guard usually used to do it, he was not obliged to do it, and did it out of courtesy; his duty being to sit behind the mail and take charge of the letter-bags, and see that his pair of pistols and blunderbuss were in such a state that they would not go off if called upon. The brace of pistols and the brass blunderbuss were always given to the guard in London with the letter-bags, and were always strapped and buckled up round the locks and trigger-guards in a sort of leather case, very securely, to prevent accidents. During the many years I drove, I never heard of one being used; nor did I ever, to my recollection, see the guard produce them, except to give them up at the Post Office at the end of his journey. I question whether they would have gone off had they been required, or whether the guard would have known how or had the pluck to 'loose them off.' Tradition said they were half-full of powder, and other dangerous matter in the shape of slugs, or lead

of some kind ; and the fact of their being buckled up
in their leather cases would have made it an affair of
time to have got them ready to bear upon Dick
Turpin, or any other 'gentleman of the road,' had
such a gentleman been in existence in the time I
write of.   There was a story on the Holyhead Mail
that a fresh guard, who did not know much of his
road or business either, I should imagine, was persuaded on his first journey to shoot at a milestone
that stood rather high on the bank on the right-hand
side of the road between Chirk and Llangollen, and
for which purpose the coachman who had gammoned
him into believing that there was a highwayman in
those parts who had stopped the mail, pulled up one
dark evening.   However, the said milestone, whether
it had been shot at or not, often served as an anecdote of the Road to credulous passengers.

' Go along, sir,' said Hodgson, the guard on the Holyhead Mail, 'if you can but get him off,' as we changed
horses at Cernioge Maur, where the offside wheeler
had jibbed and plucked, and plucked and jibbed, till
he had actually broken nearly every stitch of harness
he had on. Both traces were gone and his crupper
broken away from the pad. We had, when the other
traces broke, put him to with a chain trace, which he
had also broken. We lost above ten minutes getting
this mended at the blacksmith's shop, close by the
roadside. ' If you can but get him off, sir, never mind
the harness,' said Hodgson; 'he must go without;
we can't wait any longer; we have lost too much
time already.' Accordingly, we made a fresh attempt,
and, after sundry plunges and jibs, away went both
traces again. We, however, made a start, and I
galloped him for six miles without either traces or
crupper, and little of any kind of harness on but his

collar and the bit in his mouth. I should hardly dare relate this if a friend of mine, who is still living, and was sitting by my side on the box, would not vouch for the truth of my story. I certainly never before or since saw a horse go six miles, in any kind of convey-ance, with so little harness on him. He was a bay horse that Hodgson had bought for the man who horsed the coach; he got him in Ireland. It was the first time he had been in the mail. For two or three journeys after he was tethered with a chain like a chain cable; but start he would not till he chose; and as they always lost no end of time every day, they were obliged to draft him. Whoever had him must have got a rare bargain, for he was the most stubborn brute I ever saw or drove.

POOR little Dick's was a sad fate. He drove the mail for many years from Shrewsbury to a small village called Tinant. He was a good little fellow, always civil, always sober, always most obliging, and a friend of every one along the Road. He was a very little chap, quite the cut of a dapper little post-boy, which he had been. He was so little that, as the saying is or was, he had to get on to sixpennyworth of half-pence to look on to the top of a Stilton cheese. Be that as it may, he was strong on his box, was careful and steady as old Time, and in every way a good man in his place, and everybody respected 'little Dick Vickers.' He was very fond of fishing ; and when he had done his work, his abode at Tinant being near a small stream, he generally took his rod and beguiled his time in the 'gentle art.' In an evil and unlucky hour he was either persuaded or took the notion into his own head that he was a bit of a farmer, or would

like to be one. Accordingly, he took a small farm; he
got tired of being always by the waterside, and so took
to the land. Things seemed to go on well enough
for a time, and whilst the farm was a new toy all
seemed 'serene.' After a bit the new ploughs and
harrows got old and required repairs, his horses got
stumped up and old and required to be made into
new ones, and though the river flowed along as usual,
the money also flowed along in the wrong channel,
and poor little Dick got downcast and sighed for the
old times when he used to get off the mail, and with
a light heart, and whistling for want of thought, hurry
down to the little river which ran through his farm,
and upon which he had now to spend all his time and
money. Poor little fellow! he soon grew melancholy;
the once cheery little Dick was no longer the cheery
little Dick who drove the Holyhead Mail. He grew
more and more downcast as time went on, and one
day, sad to relate, he was found 'sus. per col.' in his
barn. The little river still flows on, and the little
trout he used to fish for still sport in the bright and
rapid stream that passes Tinant. Though the mail
he used to drive has long ceased to exist, they do say

that at times, at dusk of evening, a rumbling of wheels is heard, and that the distant sound of a mail horn may be heard, and the form of a little man may be seen with a fishing rod and basket wending his way towards the river.

Poor little Dick, as I said before, had many friends and admirers, and amongst them was the owner of Pradoe, the Honourable Thomas Kenyon, or ' His Honour,' the name he was universally known by in those days, and under which name he was beloved and respected by all who knew him. ' His Honour ' admired little Dick because he had once when a post-boy driven him faster than he ever went in his life before. The case was this, as ' His Honour ' more than once told me, and he was very fond of relating it : he was posting to London with a friend in a light barouche from his own house, Pradoe, which almost touches the Holyhead Road, between Oswestry and Shrewsbury. When he got to Shrewsbury, and pulled up at the ' Lion ' to change, ' The Wonder,' a well-known fast coach, was just ready to start. ' Dick,' said ' His Honour '—for Dick it was who was mounted and ready to start in his blue jacket, smart white cord

K

breeches, and white hat—' I wonder whether I could beat " The Wonder " into town,' meaning London. ' I should like to do it if I can. So when you get down the hill make the best of your way, and if I can only get changed and off again before " The Wonder " comes up, I think I shall do it.' ' Very good, your Honour ; I'll do my best,' said Dick, touching his hat. ' Well,' said ' His Honour,' as he pulled up at Haygate, which was the first change, and ten miles from Shrewsbury, ' you have come along, Dick ; I don't think I ever went so fast in my life ; why it's next to flying.' ' Well, we've come pretty well, I believe, sir,' said Dick ; ' but I could have come much faster, only I did not dare let the mare out,' meaning the mare he was riding ; 'as it is, she's been running away with me all the way.' But the fresh horses are in, ' The Wonder' is just appearing down the road, and ' His Honour ' is off again ; and he did beat ' The Wonder' into London, which was one of the fastest and best-appointed coaches going. It was horsed by Mr. Isaac Taylor, of the ' Lion ' at Shrewsbury, which of itself will speak for the goodness of the teams that he had anything to do with ; and I believe most others

were in no way inferior on that road. I never was on
the said 'Wonder' but once, and when I sat by the
side of Sam Hayward, from Shiffnal to Shrewsbury,
and so long as I live I shall never forget my amazement at the way he turned into the 'Lion' yard. It
was his usual way of doing business, but it astonished
me. The 'Lion' yard is just on the top of the hill,
or, as it is called in Shrewsbury, the Wyle Cop, which
is a sharpish pitch; and with a heavy load the entrance to the 'Lion' yard is so placed that it is next
to impossible to get in without coming to grief or
breaking your pole, or some such disaster. I could
not think what his manœuvre was when he hugged
the curbstone on the near side, passed the entrance
for a few yards, and turning the coach round in a
largish circle, shot into the yard. I thought at the
time that he had gone mad, and that that was his way
of turning us over; but I soon saw that he was 'master
of his fiddle,' and I found that he always played the
same tune every evening. I own I 'held on by the
brim of my hat,' and my eyelids, and everything
I could hold on by; but this was not necessary, as
he knew quite well what he was doing. Though it

was quite a new dodge to me, he was used to the performance. I must say it was very neat, quite a neat thing to do with a heavy load of passengers and luggage, but I believe it was the only way to get into the inn yard if you came up the Wyle Cop. I believe other coaches coming from the London side went in the back way, though they came out at the usual entrance.

'WILL you drive the 'bus over the bridge, sir?'
said Harry Jones, as we left the station at Bangor to
cross the Menai Bridge and join the train on the
other side, the tubular bridge not being as yet open.
'Why, thank you, Harry,' said I, 'no; I don't much
care about driving a 'bus.' 'Well, sir,' he said, 'it's
what we must all come to, you know ; you'd oblige me
by driving it across. You seed about the last of the
poor old mail, and you won't have a chance of driving
the 'bus again ; for the trains will be running through
that ere great, long, ugly iron thing,' pointing to the
tubular bridge, 'before many days is over, they tell
me.' So, to oblige poor Harry, I·drove the 'bus across
the Menai Bridge. About four years before I had the
honour of driving the 'bus; on the occasion I have
named I was driving the Holyhead Mail, and whilst
crossing the bridge I said to Jack Williams, alluding

to the railroads, 'Well, Jack, they won't manage to
get us off here in a hurry, I fancy.'   I was on my
way from fishing in Ireland, and was soon going
abroad, where I stayed nearly four years, and by the
time I came home, 'that ere great, long, ugly iron
thing,' as Harry Jones called it, was up, and all but
in working order.   No doubt a mighty work in the
way of engineering, and a great convenience to those
who frequent the Irish Mail; but of all monstrous ugly
modes of conveyance it is the most monstrously ugly,
and has utterly spoilt the fine view that used to present itself in passing over, or rather approaching, the
Menai Bridge.   No wonder that poor Harry did not
admire it in a coaching point of view, and that he
vented his wrath by calling it, what it certainly is,
' that ere great, long, ugly iron thing.'   What would
' poor dear old grandpapa' think of it, I wonder, and
how would he like the idea of shooting across an arm
of the sea, suspended between heaven and earth, with
the possibility, I hope not the probability, of the whole
thing collapsing some day or another?   On that very
line fire has done its terrible work, as in the appalling
accident near Abergele; who knows but that, some

day or another, water may not have its turn, and that the train and everybody in it may not go down with a sudden crash, and be found in 'the swillies!' It is too dreadful to think of, but still I always remember it is possible, and when I go that road I never feel 'quite the thing' till I am safe out again, and into daylight on the Anglesey side of the Straits.

I MUST now take you off the great Holyhead Road and 'the Holyhead Mail,' and introduce you to the ' Chester and Holyhead Mail,' which was a night mail.

The mail from Chester to Holyhead did not keep the same pace as that from London to Holyhead, through Shrewsbury and along the great Holyhead Road. The pace, however, of nine miles and a half an hour, including stoppages, was, I used to think, quite fast enough for a night mail; the road was not so good as the old Holyhead Road, and the mail was not so well horsed. The road, generally speaking, was rather narrow, and in many places full of twists and turns, with some sharpish hills, and on a dark night in winter you were obliged to keep your eyes well about you, or rather in front of you, and our friend in red behind had in many places to keep his horn going pretty often to warn the sleepy Welchmen that the

toll-gates must be open, and to advise the drowsy carters lugging coals (for there were several collieries in that part of the world) that the Chester Mail was on its way to Holyhead, and as these coal-carts seemed to ply more by night than by day, it was sometimes 'touch and go' to avoid spilling the coals or upsetting Her Majesty's paper-cart.

This mail used to leave the 'Feathers' Inn, at Chester, at eight o'clock ; as they say in these days, ' 8 P.M.' It was in the month of November that I met the mail at Chester, to go and shoot snipes at a friend's in Anglesey.

The mail was standing at the 'Feathers' door, horses to, and all ready for a start. ' Are you going with us this evening ?' said the guard to me. ' Yes,' I said. 'Why ? Is it a very extraordinary thing ? ' ' No, sir,' said he, 'but I'm uncommon glad to see you to-night.' 'What on earth makes you so particularly glad to see me to-night ?' 'Why, sir, to tell you the truth,' said he, ' Winterbotham's amazing fresh, and I'm sure he's not fit to drive.' 'Where is he ?' said I. ' Oh ! here he comes, sir,' and so he did, rolling about like a seventy-four in a calm, or as if he

. s

was walking with a couple of soda-water bottles tied under his feet. 'I don't know whatever we shall do with him,' said the guard, 'unless we put him inside.' It so happened that there were no inside passengers that evening, so inside we shoved him, and by the time we had got to the change, on Lord Mostyn's Training Ground, a few miles from St. Asaph, he had become pretty fairly rational, and when we looked inside to inquire after his health, though he seemed hardly to know where he was and why he had been inside, he said, 'Well, I think I'd better get outside now; I aren't used to this. Well, this is travelling like a gentleman, and inside the mail, too, to be sure. Well, I never travelled inside a mail or a coach before, and I daresay I never shall again; I don't think I like the inside of a coach much, and so I'd better get out now; it feels wonderful odd, some-how, to be inside the mail, and I really hardly know how I got here.'

I leave the Lawyer behind.

Misfortunes never come singly, they say, and in proof of this, now that Mr. Winterbotham is pretty

nearly himself again, I must go back a stage or two,
and relate another little incident that occurred on the
same journey. Our first change on leaving Chester
was at Hawarden, and there 'a gent' got up on the
mail who in his way was inclined to give some
trouble, perhaps it might be called some sport. He
had evidently 'dined,' and though not in any way
incapacitated, he was a little 'market merry,' or
'market pert,' as it is called in some counties, and
very cheery, talkative, and pleasant. I took him to
be a bagman. He was well known to Winterbotham
and the guard, and was full of his expressions of
sorrow to think that his old acquaintance Winterbotham should be drunk and incapable and put down
in the hold, instead of being on deck, as he was wont
to be. Well, at every place that we stopped he
would go in and get something to 'whet his whistle'
with, and talk and chaff with the barmaid, or do
something to cause delay. 'Come, sir,' said I, upon
one of these occasions, 'if you're coming come, for
we can't wait here all night.' Well, out he came at
last, not looking very well pleased at my remarks,
and as he was getting up on to the mail I heard

him mutter something about 'gentlemen coachmen,' of which, of course, I took no notice. 'Upon my word, sir,' I said, 'I should be sorry to leave you behind, but I shall have to do it if you delay us as you have done.' 'Leave me behind!' said he, 'I think that's more than you dare do.' 'Well, sir,' said I, 'since you fancy that, we'll see, if you delay us again; and now I promise you that if you try the same game you did at the last place I'll leave you behind; I'd leave you behind though you were Julius Cæsar or the Pope of Rome, and since you've dared me to do it I'll do it, by Jove.' Well, at the next change, which was St. Asaph, in goes my friend again. Winterbotham had become quite sane by this time, and said, 'I wish you would leave him, sir; he's always up to this game whenever he goes with us, and we've more trouble with him than enough; he'll never take advice till he is left.' The horses are to, and all ready for a start. 'Now, sir,' shouted I, 'are you going? for if you're not, I am. Castles, blow your horn, and if he don't come I'll leave him.' Castles blows. Still our friend don't make his appearance, and probably said to himself, 'Blow away, but

I'll be blowed if I come.' 'Tip him another stave, Castles, and I'm off,' said I, and, suiting the action to the word, off we went. 'Serve him right,' said Winterbotham; 'but, oh dear! won't he be in fine taking. Do you know who he is, sir?' said friend Winterbotham, who was now as sober as a judge, and sitting beside me. 'No,' said I, 'nor do I care who he is; some bagman, I suppose.' 'Oh! dear no, sir,' said he; 'he's no bagman; he's a Mr. Griffith Jones, an attorney of Carnarvon.' Well, poor Mr. Griffith Jones was left behind, and away we went without him. We arrived at Abergele and changed horses, and then on to our next change at Conway. Just as we were starting again, who should arrive in a car but the worthy attorney, having made the best of his way to catch us up. As soon as he found out the dull reality that he was really left behind he was in a tremendous fume, as may be supposed. He got upon the mail once more in anything but a plea- sant mood; he assured me that I should not play such tricks upon him with impunity; that I must be well aware that 'gentlemen coachmen' were against the law, and that he would have the 'law a-top of

me;' that he was a solicitor at Carnarvon (which I
told him I was fully aware of), and that I might
depend upon it I should hear of him again.   He
was, of course, very sulky all the way to Bangor,
where he got off to go to Carnarvon.   Whether he
ever arrived there I never heard, nor did I ever
hear of him again.   He evidently felt that I was right
and that he was wrong, and, having heard the old
saying that discretion was the better part of valour,
he thought it prudent not to show fight, and, putting
the affront into his pipe, had a quiet smoke, I conclude, when he got home.

'Hit 'em sly,' said old John Scott, as I was using all my art to boil up a trot going up Penmaen Maur; don't let 'em hear the whip, or you'll never get 'em up at all. I've tried them all manner of ways, and I've found out the way at last.' 'Well, how's that?' said I; 'if you've found out how to do it, you'd better take hold of them, for I'll be hanged if I can get them along, and we shall lose no end of time.' They were real sticky brutes, and when you hit a leader your wheelers hung back, and so all round till one got fairly tired of pitching into them.

'Ah! wait a pit, wait a pit,' said old John; 'only let me stamp the footboard.' 'Stamp the footboard,' said I; 'what will that do?' 'Wait a pit,' said John, 'wait a pit and you sall see;' and suiting the action to the word he played a sort of rat-a-tat, rat-a-tat, rat-a-tat with both his feet on the footboard. Up to their collars they sprang in a moment, and off we went up the hill right merrily. 'Well,' said I, 'that is a curious dodge ; what on earth do they think is coming ?' 'Wait a pit,' says John, 'and I'll soon let you see what is a-coming,' and stooping down and putting his hand past my legs into the boot, on the side I was sitting, he produced a most respectable and persuasive-looking ' short tommy.' ' That's what they think's a-coming,' said he. ' I'd a deal of trouble to get them along afore I got this here tommy ; but, now as I've made them used to this, as soon as I stamp the footboard they begin to expect, and if they don't go along they has it pretty sharp, and they knows it, and as soon as I begin to stamp away they goes like fun. Oh ! indeed I never has no trouble with them, now as they are used to it.'   .

A worthy, good little stout-made fellow was John Scott, a regular little Welchman, whose B was sounded like P, and when he said shall pronounced it ' sall.'

We will now go down Penmaen Maur with him, and you'll see how John used to get his glass of ale and his pipe, with the guard, at the ' Jolly Herring,'

at the bottom of Penmaen Maur. 'Send 'em along,' said John, one day. 'They'll go like fun down-hill, and I and Wallace, the guard, will have a glass of ale and a pipe of bacca at the " Jolly Herring ; " they'll go pleasant down-hill without my stamping the footboard.' So away we went, I thought rather too fast for down-hill, but John kept saying ' Send 'em along, send 'em along,' and so I did till we arrived at the small road-side inn or pot-house called the ' Jolly Herring.' There we all descended, and John Scott, Wallace, and I sat down regularly to our glass of ale and 'pipes and bacca.'

The worthy John informed me that he and Wallace did this pretty much as a matter of course if he had a 'light mail,' which meant no passengers. I don't know whether the horses used to see the joke quite in the same light, but on these occasions they always got their mouths washed out, and stood to get their breaths for a few minutes. What the authorities at the General Post Office might have thought, I suppose, never entered John or the guard's heads.

T

CRUELTY TO DUMB ANIMALS.

' Upon my word,' said a gentleman who was sitting beside me as I was driving the Chester and Holyhead Mail up St. George's Hill, close to Kinmel Park, between Abergele and St. Asaph; ' upon my word, it's a shame to punish horses so ; it's downright cruelty to flog horses in that manner.' It was what might be called cruelty to dumb animals ; but what was I to do ? I had to keep nine miles and a half an hour, including stoppages, and St. George's Hill was about as steep as a church spire, and a long hill into the bargain.

My team consisted of a lot of old screws, belonging to a Mr. Green of St. Asaph, who horsed the mail, and was famed for horsing it worse than any man on the road ; they were as sticky as treacle and had hides like a rhinoceros, for no amount of double thong, or anything I could offer them, had any more effect upon them than it would have had they been

made of india-rubber. 'It's a shame, by Jove it is,' said the 'gent,' 'and it ought to be reported to the Society for the Prevention of Cruelty to Animals.' At this remark Charlie Harper, who drove the Chester and Holyhead Mail, and afterwards was on the London and Holyhead Mail, seemed delighted, and said, ' I wish you would do it, sir; I wish you'd inform the Society; you'd do a public service. If Mr. Reynardson did not lump them, I should have to do it; so it comes to the same thing. It is a shame; but what's one to do? The time must be kept by some means; and the Post Office, I dare say, don't care who lumps Mr. Green's horses, so long as the mail keeps its time.' Some time after this occurrence the said Mr. Green was informed against.

And to the delight of Charlie Harper, and all others who had to drive Mr. Green's bad horses, he had to pay something considerable, though I forget what it was, to say nothing of a long reprimand and jobation from the ' Denbighshire Beaks.'

It must not be supposed from what I have said that *all* the teams on the Chester and Holyhead Road were equally bad; there were some good ones, and had it not been so we could not have done our nine and a half miles an hour, for there were some stiffish pitches along the road, and some of them so much so that our 'Friend in Red' would at times take the opportunity of stretching his legs up some of the steepest of them. The road I am speaking of was not like that made by the great 'Telford' through Shrewsbury, where every yard was trotting ground. There was, however, nothing *insurmountable* to a good team, who stuck their toes well into the ground, and 'threw their hearts' into the work they had before them.

I MUST ask your indulgence whilst I take you off the Holyhead Road and transport you into Italy and the St. Gothard Pass, where took place a scene so terrible, and which might have proved so dreadful, that at this moment I dread to recall the occurrence to my mind.

Soon after the scene with the Holyhead and Chester Mail, when the gentleman pronounced the treatment of Mr. Green of St. Asaph's horses to be a fitting subject for the attention of the Society for the Prevention of Cruelty to Animals, I left England, and went *via* Switzerland to Italy, and got as far as Rome. Before leaving England, being full of visions of driving my own coach all over the world, I bought a large yellow coach, a regular 'drag,' and four-horse harness. I started with my family, meaning most fully to buy horses on the other side of the water. I grew, however, faint-hearted, and my pockets got low, and when the wheels required greasing I could not find the wherewith to grease them. So I posted and travelled 'voiturier' with my great yellow coach, sometimes lugging my harness with me, and sometimes sending it by 'roulage,' till I thought I should have gone mad with the bother and trouble I had. Sometimes I lost it altogether, and sometimes the Douaniers at the frontiers detained it, wondering what I could want with harness and no horses. They gave me all sorts of trouble; still the harness stuck to me, and we got to Milan. From Milan I was persuaded by a friend to go on to Rome, and the harness was again sent by 'roulage' to Rome, where I was quite determined to get some horses, 'coûte qui coûte.' When I reached Rome no harness had come, and when it did come the idiots—for I can call them nothing else—would not let it enter the 'Holy City.' It remained in the Custom-house for some weeks, and no power would induce the officials to loose their hold of it. It was a 'contraband of war,' and they would not let me pay duty for it, or let me even see it. At last I got an audience of a good-natured old cardinal, Cardinal Tosti, who, upon my giving him the 'word of a Britisher ' that I would not sell it, liberated my harness. What to do with it when I had it again I knew not. I could not find any horses : and if I had, I had not the cash to pay for them, and so, after much bother and perplexity of mind, I sent the infernal harness all the way back to England ; and when I got home had it made up into two pairs of pair-horse harness, and a dearish two pairs of harness it was to me. Well, off we started from Rome with a voiturier and four of the best little grey ponies, for they were nothing' else, for Milan. With our pile of luggage and ourselves, and our children and servants, we were such a load that our courier insisted upon my buying a fourgon. This I did, and away we went.

Having arrived at the last village on the Italian side of the St. Gothard, and just before we began to descend the Pass, a German gentleman, who was posting with his wife and children in a large open calash, was very anxious to pass us ; but we would not allow him to do this. His postillion kept pressing upon us till we got to the top of the St. Gothard. He was rather annoying to us, and we begged him to desist. The courier told him that as we must be in time for the boat at Fluellyn, which is a village on the Lake of Lucerne, he would also be there in time, without making himself disagreeable.

When we got to the top of the hill, or Pass, we put the skid on the coach, and also on the fourgon, in which the courier and my children were, and began the descent, the fourgon leading the way. On looking round to see where the troublesome carriage was, we saw the owner of it walking down the hill, the lady's maid sitting on the box and holding the reins; the skid chain had broken, and the postillion or driver went back to pick the skid up. He had to go some little distance, and was coming back with it when the horses moved on. Finding no one holding them, they got into a trot, and, being frightened, got into a gallop, and came down the hill as hard as they could lay legs to the ground. They passed my coach on the off-side within a hair's breadth, but did not touch it. Our voiturier had just time to draw a little on one side as he saw them coming. They passed the fourgon, in which the children and courier were, on the near side, and between it and a wall. On the

other side there was a precipice of hundreds of yards
in depth. The carriage just shaved the fourgon on
the near side, and went on its way headlong, swing-
ing from side to side of the road, as if it must turn
over at any moment. There seemed to be no mode
of escape, nor the slightest chance for the maid on
the box or the ladies and children inside. Their
doom seemed certain, and nothing but a miracle, as it
seemed, could prevent their going over the precipice
and being dashed to pieces. Away they went as hard
as their horses' legs could carry them, round a corner,
and were lost to our sight. We went on slowly, and
made sure that we should see the calash and everybody belonging to it dashed to atoms far below us in
the terrible chasm, composed of nothing but solid rock
and large stones. To our surprise, when round the
corner, we saw the calash at some little distance hanging over the precipice. On arriving at the scene of
this great and providential escape, we found the poor
German lady and her children safe, and the carriage
jammed against one of the large stones that were put
on the side next the precipice for a kind of protection.
The off fore-wheel of the carriage was actually hang-

ing over the precipice, and in half a foot more the carriage and all would have been over it. The poor maid had been thrown over the wall on the near side, and had hurt her leg, the reins having been entangled round one of them. As soon as I found that the party in the calash were all safe, and that I could do nothing to assist them, except sending a carriage to take them down to the inn at the bottom of the hill, I put the poor maid into my coach and took her to the inn. I put her leg into a bucket of hot water, and did all I could for her till her master and mistress arrived.

I shall never forget that scene—the calash clashing with my fourgon, in which my children were, the calash rolling from side to side of the road, the women inside screaming, the poor husband in a frantic state, rushing along the road after his wife and children, with his hands clasped and such a look of despair as I hope never to see again. How the horses had managed to break away from the carriage without upsetting it is a perfect marvel. The shock, at the pace they were going, must have been tremendous when the wheel came against the stone post close to the edge of the precipice, and had torn off the splinter-bar. This was, no doubt, the salvation of those in the calash, and on looking down the zigzag road the four horses were to be seen more than a mile away, looking no larger than four ants, galloping headlong round the turns in the road, on their way to their stables at the inn at the bottom of the St. Gothard, where we found them. We arrived with the poor lady's maid, with her sprained and badly-bruised leg, which luckily was the extent of the mischief, nothing being broken. The gentleman, I hear, in remembrance of, and in gratitude for, the miraculous escape of his wife and family, has built a small shrine or chapel on the spot where the scene took place.

When I and my family and the yellow coach got safely back to England, not without much regret, I decided to sell the old yellow companion of my travels. It was a very good coach, and before leaving England had cost me 113 sovereigns. I thought that no end of people would like to buy the article, and I held out stoutly for eighty pounds for it. No one seemed, however, to want it. I came

down in my price ; still everybody did not run after it,
as I had hoped and expected. I advertised it ; I stood
it at livery ; I put it in the Pantechnicon for many
weeks, at half-a-crown a week ; I put it to stand at
Tattersall's for many more weeks to the 'same tune.'
At last I grew desperate and reckless, and having
consulted Messrs. Tattersall, they advised me to 'sell it
for what it would fetch.' Accordingly there appeared
an advertisement stating that a yellow four-horse
coach, built by Cooke and Rowley, the property of
a gentleman who had no further use for it, would be
sold without reserve on such a day. I took the precaution to take away a very good pair of lamps I had
had made for it and put in the old ones, and begged
Mr. Tattersall to do his best for me. He used all
his persuasive eloquence, which we all know was great,
and having brought all bidders to a stand-still, he pronounced the following : 'For the last time going for six
guineas ; for the last time at six guineas ; it's to be
sold. Oh! gentlemen, you'll surely not let such a
coach as that go for six guineas! Have you all done,
gentlemen ? for the last time at six guineas ; going for
six guineas, for the last time,' and bang goes the ham-

mer.   He gave me a cheque for six pounds, keeping
the shillings, as is usual on such occasions, for the
firm of Tattersall and Company.

So ended my yellow coach!

MOPING A HOT LEADER.

'SPOT' AND THE 'NETTLE' COACH.

'WHAT have you got here, Shaw?' said I, addressing
the coachman of the 'Nettle,' as the fresh team was
being put in at Oswestry, the subject of my inquiries
being the off-side leader, a thoroughbred, upstanding,
wild-looking, dark brown horse, all over white ticks,
or flea-bites, with a large piece of leather over his
eyes, like half of a black coal-scuttle. 'What on earth
have you got that piece of machinery on for?' 'Well,'
said Shaw, 'he's a very queer sort of a chap that, and
if he had not been a real "rum 'un" I reckon we
should never have had him in the coach; he's a good
horse, however, for all that; and now that I know
him and he knows me, we never fall out, and are on
the best of terms, and I don't know that I ever drove
a better leader. I've only had him four or five journeys; he was a bit troublesome at first, and raked and

pulled in style, I can promise you, for he did not seem
to like not being first. He's done a bit of racing in
his time, and ran at Chester last year ; he's full of
mettle, as hot as the d——l, and as shy as a trout.
I hear he always was so. He belonged to a bagman
who used to travel this road ; but about ten days
since he ran away with his trap, kicked it all to pieces,
killed the bagman, and galloped along the road half-
way to Shrewsbury. He's terribly shy of harness now,
and sometimes gives a deal of trouble, and pulls and
frets and shies at everything ; so now I find it's
always the best plan to "mope him."' Some time since
I saw this in the 'Field' : 'Can any of your corre-
spondents inform me what is meant by "moping a hot
leader ?"' Thought I to myself, if you had ever driven
'Spot' in the 'Nettle' coach you would have known.
I can't say he actually ran away with me at the time
I mention, because, as I had been 'put up to the time
of day' by Shaw Evans, I was on the look-out, and
treated him very 'gingerly ;' but this I can say, that
I could not hold him a yard from Oswestry to Chirk,
and he was ready to run away at any moment. It's
a horrid bore being run away with, by-the-bye. 'Spot'

and I, however, became the greatest friends, and after
our first drive he never pulled an ounce, and was
one of the finest leaders I ever drove, if not the
finest.

GAMMONING THE WELCHMAN.

'DEAR heart alive!' said a respectable-looking old man to me one day as I was driving the 'Nettle' coach between Chirk and Oswestry, and just coming in sight of the Brython Hills—'dear a me; why, them hills don't seem half so big or so high as they used to be when I was a boy.' 'You seem to know this part of the country, or to have known it in former days,' I said. 'Ah! indeed, I used to know it well "onste," when I was younger; but I have seen a deal since I was last in these parts. I've been away in America these thirty years or more, and I suppose I've forgot like that the hills are not so big as I used to think them when I was a little chap and lived in this part of the country. To be sure, I've seen many bigger mountains since I've been away, but I did fancy somehow that them hills used to be bigger. I only landed at Liverpool last night, and I'm going to see my old friends in Welchpool.'

X

'Oh! sir,' I said, 'if you are going to Welchpool your friends there will be able to tell you much more than I can about the Brythen Hills; but I don't wonder at your thinking them smaller than they used to be. The fact is, they are not so high as they used to be before you left these parts, and the people about Welchpool have not been idle since you left the country. You will find many improvements, and amongst others this, that they have taken off the top of the large hill in front of you, and which you justly remark seemed larger; and they have filled up the valley you may remember on the other side of it, and this will fully account for its looking smaller, and will prove that your memory has been good as to its former size.' Well, my friend the Welchman opened his eyes, taking everything I said for gospel, observing that England was a wonderful place, and that industry and improvements would never cease. I left the coach at Llanymyneck, near which little town I was then living, and he went on his way to Welchpool, where he would, in all probability, relate his little adventure, and very possibly afford some amusement to his friends.

Perhaps more by luck than judgment, I never came to any great grief in my coaching days; I never upset a coach, and I never was upset by anyone else; I never killed anyone; and I never was killed myself, which I have often thought a wonderful fact, for I have often seen queer things happen, and have had various 'touch and goes,' which even now make my hair stand on end; that is to say, the little of it that remains. I believe I never killed or ran over anything that I ought not but once, and then I ran over and killed a pig. Poor 'Mr. Wiggins!' he was turned into pork at a moment's notice in a way he could hardly have expected, but which, perhaps, was quite as much to his taste and quite as dignified as being confined in a sty, and fed up for weeks, and doomed at last to undergo the process of being shaved at Christmas and turned into pork pies or sausages.

It happened thus. I was driving the 'Nettle'

coach, which ran from Welchpool to Liverpool. I had
a real good load, four in and twelve out, and luggage
in proportion, when going through the toll-bar close
to Llanymyneck, near which place I had a friend
living whose house I was going to look at, with the
intention of hiring it. Just as I got my leaders well
through the toll-bar, who should pop out but my
friend 'Mr. Wiggins' right under the near wheel of
the coach. I shall never forget the sound of the wheel
cutting through him ; it was just the sound that would
be produced by driving over a washerwoman's wicker
clothes-basket, or something like the horrible crunch
that is heard in one's head when a double tooth is
being wrenched out. I'd half a mind to pull up to
see if the poor fellow required any assistance ; but the
guard said, 'Never mind him, sir; he's as dead as
mutton.' And as the 'Nettle' was then running opposition to the 'Royal Oak,' the pace was too good to stop
and inquire after him. It so happened that this took
place on a Saturday ; I got off at my friend's house
about two miles further on, and on Sunday went with my
friend to Llanymyneck Church, and had to pass through
the said toll-bar. On our return we went into the toll-

bar with an excuse to get a light for a cigar, and there, spread out on a clean white tablecloth, were evident signs of my acquaintance of yesterday, cut up and looking very like very nice, pork. 'The deuce take it,' said I, 'you surely don't kill pigs on a Sunday in this country!' 'No, sir,' said the toll-bar keeper; 'it's a pig that met with a little bit of an accident yesterday; the coach went over it and killed it. But it will make a very nice bit of pork for all that, and I don't see that it will be much the worse, though it aren't perhaps quite so fat as it might be to kill in the usual way.'

'Did the coach really kill the pig?' said I. 'I suppose that it was all the coachman's fault, and that he was driving too fast, or something of that kind.' 'Well, no, sir; I don't see how anyone was to blame this time,' he said. 'To be sure they do race a bit sometimes, the "Oak" and "Nettle" do; but I don't see that the coachman or anyone was to blame but the pig himself. I'll tell you how it was, sir; my missis oftentimes gives the pig a bit of victuals inside that rail which you see is broken,' pointing to a part of the garden fence which ran up close to the

door, and out of which just enough rails were broken
out to admit poor piggy; 'and just as the coach was
going through the gate out he pops right under the
wheel, and, to be sure, there was no help for him,
and the coach did fairly cut him in two.' Introducing
me at the same time to the piece of his ribs that the
wheel had gone over, he held it up for my edification.
'Well,' I said, 'it couldn't be helped, I suppose. What
might such a pig as that be worth?' 'Well, sir, it
might be worth a couple of pounds; it's only a little
'un yet, do you see.' 'Well,' I said, 'you're a good
fellow for not blaming the coachman; here's a sovereign
for you to get some apple-sauce to eat with him. I
was driving, as it so happened, and if you'd blamed
the coachman I should have kept my sovereign in
my pocket.'

He seemed astonished and not a little pleased at
the transaction. I hired my friend's house for three
or four years, and often as I passed the toll-bar I
went in and lit my cigar, and had a little chaff about
the 'gentleman coachman' turning pork butcher. I
need not say that during the time I lived there we
were sworn friends; and often as I drove the coach

through the toll-bar, when he touched his hat to me, I acknowledged it by 'Mind your pigs.' Just as I am finishing my story of the pig at Llanymyneck toll-bar, I see in the 'Times' the following :—

'ACCIDENT ON A RAILWAY.—A signalman in the employ of the Cambrian Railway, named John Whittington, was cut to pieces by a train near Llanymyneck station yesterday afternoon.'

I believe the station is within a few yards of where the pig catastrophe took place, and it is what the Yankees call 'a caution' that at the time I am writing of the 'Nettle' coach and poor pig I should see the familiar name of Llanymyneck, and read of a much more sad accident on the railroad at the same fatal spot.

'PETER HILTON' AND THE STRANGE GENTLEMAN.

'HALLO, Peter! How about that "strange gentleman?"' said a brother coachman as he pulled up along-
side the above-named Peter Hilton, who drove the
'Hirondelle' from Shrewsbury to Birkenhead, from
which place the passengers crossed by a ferry-boat
to Liverpool. 'All along with that strange gentleman's driving, eh, Peter!' 'If that is all you've got
to say,' said Peter, 'you'd better mind your own business.' This was a mighty sore subject with Peter,
who at the best of times was not famed for his
affable manners, if anything put him out. He was
not very fond of chaff; and the incident I am about to
relate afforded a grand subject for banter on the road
and with many of his brother coachmen, who all knew
me pretty well. The facts were these: Peter, for
some reasons best known to himself, for I could never
make them out, was not vastly fond of me. I knew

him less than any coachman on the road, and certainly had never given him any cause for either liking
or disliking me. He never much approved of my
driving, though he knew I was in the habit of driving
any of the coaches out of Shrewsbury and elsewhere
in that part of the country. It happened one day
that Mr. Isaac Taylor, of the Lion Inn, in Shrewsbury, who horsed most of the coaches, was in the
yard when the 'Hirondelle' was about to start. He
had given me leave to drive any team of his, and
seemed surprised not to see me lay hold of the reins
and mount the rostrum. 'Aren't you going to drive,
sir?' said he; 'you'll find them a fairish team, I think.'
'Well, to tell you the truth,' said I, 'Peter Hilton
don't seem much to like my driving.' 'Never mind
Peter Hilton,' said Mr. Taylor, 'jump up, sir; I'll
make it all right,' calling out at the same time,
'Hilton, Mr. Reynardson is going to work to-day.'
'Very well, sir, if you like it,' said Peter, looking as
sulky as he could look, and he could look it to per-
fection. Off we started; a horrid day, I well remember, raining and blowing great guns, so that I could
hardly keep the horses in the road, the wind dead in

my teeth, and the rain driving up the road, till reins, whip, and everything else were as wet and soddened as if they had been boiled or were made of tripe.

Having arrived at Wrexham, where a dog-cart was waiting for me to take me to a friend's house about two miles distant, down I jumped, gave Peter a 'douceur,' which I hoped would make him think better of me for the time to come, and said, 'Good day, Peter; don't look so cross. I'll come and drive for you again some day ere very long,' and with this I jumped into the dog-cart, and was off before the horses were out of the coach. Some time afterwards I met my old friend Mr. Kenyon, or 'His Honour,' as he was always called. 'Hallo, old friend,' said he, much to my surprise; 'how came you to let Peter Hilton's horses get away from you the other day?' Of course I was all amazement, never having heard of any occurrence that could give rise to the speech. 'I don't know what you mean,' I said. 'I never let Peter Hilton's horses get away, nor did I hear of anything of the kind. I can't make out what you mean.' 'Why,' said his Honour, 'did not you drive the 'Hirondelle' on such a day from Shrewsbury, and

did not they run off with the coach from Wrexham?'
To this I replied that I had never heard of anything
of the kind having taken place, and stated, as I have
before said, that as soon as I got off the coach at
Wrexham, being wet and miserable, I got into the dog-
cart and made the best of my way to my friend's
house, before the horses were even taken out of the
coach. 'Well, Peter said you did, and it's all over
the country; so, as you did not do it, you will
know what to say if any one chaffs you about it.' It
would seem that while they were putting the horses
to at the Feathers Inn, at Wrexham, my friend Peter
and the three or four passengers that were on the
coach—for I remember we had only a light load
that day—slipped into the inn to 'whet their whistles,'
and Wrexham was famous for its good ale in those
days. From some cause the horsekeeper left the
horses for a moment, and when he returned, to his
surprise, he found the coach gone, and, to his greater
surprise, friend Peter and his passengers in the bar.
The horses had started off first in a walk, then in a
trot, then got into a gallop, and away they went with
the empty coach at any pace you like to call it, till

they got to the bottom of Marford Hill, about five
miles from Wrexham. How they were stopped, why
they stopped, whether they were stopped by anyone,
or whether they stopped of their own accord, I never
heard; but stop they did, and the coach and horses
came to no grief. Will Jones, who was driving the
coach from Liverpool to Wrexham, met them about
half-way down the hill, and seeing something was
wrong, there being no one on the coach, pulled
almost out of the road, and avoided being run into.
He said they were going a real good pace, and he
could not for the life of him make out what could.be
up till he got to Wrexham, and found how matters
stood. Peter Hilton, to get the blame off his own
shoulders and avoid the chaff which he must go
through, and thinking that he should never hear any
more of it, laid it to my driving, and said, 'Oh! it
was all along with that strange gentleman driving.'
He was soon, however, found out, and the chaff he
got was without end. He never passed a coach without being reminded of the strange gentleman. ' How
about that strange gentleman, Peter; have you seen
him lately ?' used constantly to be thrown in his face.

It was about this time, but now so long since that I forget the exact year, that I went over to stay a night at 'His Honour's' to meet Sir Henry Peyton— I mean the Sir Henry Peyton of old, with his yellow coach and his greys. He would, in these days, be called one of the Old School, and slow. So he might be; but he was the picture of a man on the box, and though he never drove very fast no one knew better what he was doing than 'Sir Henry.' His horses were always better put together than any other team, and he was all over a workman. He looked it, and his looks did not belie him.

We were sitting after dinner discussing a bottle of Raike's port. Sir Henry was a big man and liked the better part of a bottle of port, and Raike's port in that day was 'nulli secundus.'

'I don't know why it is that horses always seem

to go better at night than they do in the day-time,'
said I to 'His Honour;' 'but I always fancy they do.'
'Don't you know why that is?' said 'His Honour,'
'what say you, Peyton? I daresay you can give
a good reason.' 'No, by Jove, I can't,' said the
Baronet. 'I really believe that they do, though. I do
think that they always go better at night, but I never
could make out a really good reason for it.' 'Well
then,' said 'His Honour,' 'I'll tell you, and I never
could make it out till Chester Billy told me.' One
word 'en passant' about 'Chester Billy.' He was a
character in his way, and a sort of tame cat at 'His
Honour's,' being an old coachman, and a great ally
of mine host's. He used to drive a coach from
Shrewsbury to Chester, and did and said pretty much
what he liked when at 'His Honour's.' At Chester
he was called 'Shrewsbury Billy,' and at Shrewsbury
he was called 'Chester Billy,' and was as well known
by the two names at the two different towns as the
town-clock itself. 'Well,' said 'His Honour,' 'I'll
tell you. One night after dinner I got on the mail;
the horses seemed to go so well and merrily that I
turned to Billy, and said, "Hang me, Billy, if I can

make it out, but horses always seem to go better at
night than they do in the day. I've tried to account
for it, but I never could satisfactorily." "Why, I am
surprised at you," said Billy; "do you mean that you
really don't know that?" "Why, of course I don't,"
said "His Honour," "or I should not ask you."
"Well, then," said Billy, "if you want to know the
real reason, it is because you have had your dinner."
Of course, this must be the reason, and not a bad
one either. I remember poor old Sir Henry was
mightily pleased at this bit of information.

I MENTIONED in a former chapter, where I related
the anecdote of the killing of a pig at Llanymyneck
toll-bar, that I had been most fortunate in never
having come to serious grief on a coach, and that,
with the exception of this little *contretemps*, having a
horse down occasionally, and such trifles, my coaching
days had passed off as serenely as one could well
expect. I often think that, considering the heavy
loads on the coaches and the pace on the mails, this
fact was a great subject for congratulation. I very
nearly, however, had a real good accident, which may
be worth relating. For this purpose I shall ask indulgence whilst I take you off the regular road for a
short time, and relate how on a private drag I might,
with others, have come to sad grief, had not everything turned up right, and just as it did. I started
from a friend's house near Wrexham, in North Wales,
on a gentleman's coach, to go a journey of about

forty miles. I was to drive the first half of the road
and my friend the other half. We had a good load
of passengers, and, as there were ladies, of course a
good load of luggage. We got safely down a very
steep hill close to the house, and trotted away very
comfortably along a flat piece of ground in the park,
till we came to within a short distance of a very
steep pitch called the Lodge Hill, leading to the Lodge
gates. 'By Jove, I must spring them a bit,' I said,
'or we shall never get up the Lodge Hill.' I was
just off, when my friend, to whom the horses and
whole turnout belonged, said : 'Oh ! dear no ; pray
don't ; let them go quietly ; old Miller has been rather
ailing, and was bled yesterday, and you'd better not
hurry him,' meaning an old white horse that ran off-
side wheeler. The team was a grey team, with a
nervous, fidgetty, active little horse, called 'Grimaldi,'
tethered to the off-side leader by a check rein. There
was no vice about him, but he was a fire-away little
fellow, and at times given to rake a little, and therefore my friend usually drove him with a check rein
coupled to the off-side horse. According to the
orders I had received, we were going up the sharp

pitch at a dead pull and a foot's pace, when all of a
sudden, just as we got under a large spreading oak
tree, whose branches hung over the road, so that
there was hardly room for our heads without ducking,
the off-leader choked and went down bang on his
head, pulling Grimaldi down with him, broke the
check rein, and pulled the tongue of one of the
buckles on the coupling rein through the buckle. Up
jumped Grimaldi, and being, like the famous clown of
that name, very active on his legs, he went up the
side of the bank and then down again into the road,
then up the bank again, looking as wild as a hawk,
and at one time I really thought he was coming to
sit beside me on the box. The grooms jumped down,
my friend jumped down, and made the best of his
way up the bank, and everybody would have jumped
down if they could ; but the scrimmage was very
quick, and there was no time for anything, and matters
were getting serious. The coach was running back,
and the brutes of wheelers would not help me, and
kept backing. I was under the tree, and, from the
branches almost touching my head, I could not use
my whip to keep them up ; it was impossible to ad-

minister any persuasion in the double thong line. All
of a sudden the two leaders turned short round,
having got upon their legs again. The bars flew up,
caught the pole-hook cross-ways, and pulled it out as
straight as a kitchen skewer; the bars, all three, of
course, fell down, and dangled about their heels.
They set to kicking, and having no kind of command
of them from the coupling reins being broken, I
thought it advisable to get rid of them if possible.
So I divided my leading reins from my wheelers, and
when they made a plunge I dropped the leading
reins on to the wheelers' terrets and let them go. I
was uncommonly glad to see them free of me and the
coach, and galloping away across the meadow with
the bars dangling behind them and the reins trailing
along on the ground. Had not the pole-hook bent
and let the bars go free, I know not what would
have become of us; as it was, all went as well as
could be expected under such circumstances. Had
the pole-hook behaved otherwise than it did, I conclude we should have had the pleasure of being run
away with across the meadow, and should possibly
ultimately have found ourselves in the river which ran

hard by; for from the fact of the coupling reins being
broken, and the tongue having been pulled through
the buckle, all the steering power was gone from the
'man at the helm.' Whilst the scrimmage was going
on, the wheelers, who had behaved very well on the
whole, had backed one wheel against the bank, and
there we were, half across the road. It did not,
therefore, take much time or trouble to turn round
entirely and go to the bottom of the hill, where I
pulled up, and having taken the longest breath I ever
took in my life, or ever hope to take again, I congratulated myself and the two or three passengers
that had remained on the coach that matters were no
worse, and that we were 'all alive and kicking.' I think
I hear some one say, 'Were you not in a horrid
funk?' to which I answer, 'Yes, in a horrid funk.' As
soon as I had pulled up I was in a horrid funk, but
there was no time to funk whilst the scrimmage was
actually going on. It was a real 'quick thing,' and
no time was allowed for either thinking or funking.
The whole affair, though it takes a good while to
describe upon paper, was performed in an incredibly
short space of time, and so long as I live I shall

never forget the whole scene. The four horses at
one time were so mixed together that they seemed
to be tied in a knot. I have many times since
thought the affair over, and have asked myself this
question : Should such an accident occur again, and,
knowing what you do, how would you act? and I
have always come to this conclusion, that under the
same circumstances I should do as I then did; and
I don't see what else I could have done. Had I,
however, to go through it again, knowing what I do,
I should insist upon driving the horses in the way
I chose and thought best. I should have run them
pretty fast at the hill, which after all was only a
sharp pitch, instead of going as slow up it as if we
were going to a funeral. Had I sprung them a little,
I am persuaded I should have got up without anything going wrong; but as the coach and horses and
everything belonged to my friend, and as he was
sitting beside me on the box, and as I was only his
'curate,' I could not help myself.

Reader, did you ever 'sup off pork,' and have a
nightmare in which you fancied you were driving
along pleasantly, till all of a sudden you came to a

hill, which gradually grew steeper and steeper as you went up it, till your horses struggled to get up it; and as it grew steeper and steeper, they struggled and struck their toes into the hill, scrambling and struggling till it became so steep that you were hardly able to sit upon your box. Still they scrambled and struggled, the hill getting more and more perpendicular, till at last there was nothing to be seen but the horses above you, and down they all came with a last struggle and a horrible crash upon you. If you ever have 'supped off pork,' and suffered such an indigestion as to produce such a nightmare; if you have felt this, this was something like the kind of feeling in going np the Lodge Hill.

But you will say, perhaps, Why, if you found that the coach was retrograding down the hill, and if, on account of the overhanging oak tree, you were not able to use your whip and keep your wheelers up to their work, why did you not put on your patent break to stop the coach? To this I answer, In those days there were no such things invented as patent breaks; and if there had been I could not have found hands to use one. I had only two hands, and upon the occasion I

have named they were both in great request. Depend
upon it, that unless a man has more than one pair of
hands, if he gets into a real good scrawl, he has no hand
at liberty to use a patent break. A patent break is
doubtless a clever invention, and for hilly roads in a
country like Scotland, and elsewhere, most useful; but
for ordinary roads I see but little use for it, unless it
is put behind the coach, and is used by the guard, or
the servant doing duty for the guard, and who, in the
ordinary way of things, would attend to the putting on
and taking off the skid. It may be useful sometimes,
but in most cases where it might be of the greatest use
it is utterly useless and out of place; for I will defy
any man, if he gets suddenly into a serious mess, to
keep one of his hands at liberty to work his patent
break. If the break is behind, the servant can put it
on at a moment's notice; but the coachman in a scrape
wants both his hands, and many is the time that I
should have been very glad of three, or perhaps four.
The handle of a break is an ugly thing sticking up
by the side of the box; it is much in your way when
getting up, and when you are up seems always to be
in the wrong place. It is a bad practice to be always

putting on and taking off the break down every little
pitch in the road; it teaches your horses not to hold,
than which there cannot be a greater fault. A good
pair of wheelers, if taken steadily off the crown of the
hill, will hold almost anything in reason ; and unless
the hill is very steep, and there is not a bit of gravel
or loose stone to run your wheel on, your break is a
nuisance, or next to a nuisance, and it in a great degree
spoils the look of a coach. Let me not be misunder-
stood. I do not say that a patent break is not a
useful article at times. The use of it and the abuse
of it are two different things. Should your pole-chains
by any chance break or come unhooked, going down a
hill, a break may be the saving of you. Should a horse
come down going down-hill, or going up-hill either,
put on your break, if you can find hands for it at such
a time, till you can get him on his legs again. It is, I
own, a better plan than having to put a stone under
your wheel, but your 'shooter' should do this; your
man behind, or whoever is acting as guard, should
attend to your break.

Never let anything tempt you to put a piece of
brick under your wheel. I once saw this done in a

town where there happened to be a brick close at
hand; the pressure of the wheel and the weight of
the coach broke the brick, and we were very nearly
having an accident. I think I hear you say, Why, a
man must be a born fool to think of putting a brick
under a coach wheel. So he may, but I've seen it
done; and what is more, I've seen a lot of coal-trucks
on a railway siding and on an incline only scotched
by a piece of brick. I mentioned the subject to a
porter, and he said it was 'all right.'

Thus I must own that a patent break may be, and
is, a useful thing, if used when necessary and with
moderation. But to see a man on a coach pumping
away at his break-handle, as if he was filling a bucket
in a stable yard, whenever there is a little pitch in the
road, and his leaders, with their traces as tight as the
strings on Bottesini's double-bass fiddle, pulling down-
hill as if they were going up, is not workmanlike, and
is enough to call the spirits of Sir Henry Peyton and
his greys, or 'His Honour' (the Honourable Thomas
Kenyon) and his chestnuts, with their yellow coaches,
from their resting-places.

If you will kindly keep your eyes about you, good

A A

reader, you will perceive that what I have said is a
fact; and that to such a pitch has the patent break
come in these days, that many a gentleman's coachman, not content with using it at every little pitch
along the road, positively puts it on when he pulls
up at the hall-door on his arrival at home. How he
manages it I hardly know, for as he generally has his
reins in two hands, he ought to have at least three
to do it neatly. I fear that my notions of the patent
break may appear rather antiquated to those of the
present day, so I will say no more, but crave their
forgiveness and return to the Road.

THE coachman of the present day has no idea of what a coach-load of former days was; he could have no idea of what a coach was doomed to carry, unless he had been there to see. In the first place, there were four inside and twelve out, exclusive of the coachman and guard. The fore-boot was full of small parcels, the hind-boot was the same; the roof of the coach was piled up as high as it could be to allow of its passing under the archway of the inn; and boxes and carpet-bags, gun-cases, hampers, and every description of luggage for the sixteen people who were inside and out, were heaped up and hanging over the sides of the roof, which was all covered down with a tarpaulin, and securely strapped down with a broad leather strap. It was wonderful to behold, and wonderful to imagine how it could all be stowed away.

On the very lamp-irons you would often see game

baskets hung, and hares and pheasants dangling down.
Under the coach there was often swung a 'cradle,'
into which various things which could go nowhere else
were put; in fact, the whole packing of a heavy load
was marvellous, and what none but a guard of the
olden time dare attempt. In spite of all this heavy
loading there was seldom a-break-down, and really not
often an accident of any kind; and on an opposition
coach this was a wonder, for the pace that on some
occasions was kept up was 'no joke,' such galloping
was there one against another, such 'corner-creeping,'
and such machinations to be first. Many a time have
I seen a coach pulled up, and changed, and off again,
without the coachman ever getting off his box; the
horsekeeper, or one of them—for there were generally
two or three—throwing a rein over the whip as he drew
them through the terrets, and the coachman catching
hold of them by lifting his whip up to his hand. There
was no time for going into the bar, and getting a bit of
bread and cheese and a glass of ale, on these fast occasions. The barmaid would sometimes have the useful
articles on a tray and hand them up to a hungry passenger; but there was no getting down. There was

no time to talk to and chaff with the pretty barmaid
in the bar; the change used to be effected in an incredibly short space of time, and you had just time to
swallow your glass of ale. That was about all the
time that you had, and with a 'right' from the guard
you were off again at once, and had to eat your bread
and cheese as you went along. 'Now, Jack,' or Will, or
whatever the guard's name was, the coachman would
say, if it was night or early morning, and the lamps
were lit, 'Blessed if I did not see their lamps, and
they are coming along, I promise you; just put something over your boot-lamp, and I'll spring them a bit
when we get round the turn.' It may seem odd in these
days to talk of a lamp to the hind-boot, but on fast
coaches it was a wonderfully handy thing for a guard,
who had often to get small parcels out of the hind-boot;
but it was a regular 'tell-tale' to the coach behind you,
if the coachman caught a glimpse of his adversary's hind-
boot lamp. Such were some of the dodges used in
days gone by to keep first. There was a good deal
of excitement in the sort of thing, and, I suspect, a little
danger also. A coach with a full load, and particularly
an 'opposition coach,' required some care and skill to

keep it right end upwards; and I have often wondered
that there were not more accidents, for at times, in
galloping with a top-heavy load, they would swing a
bit, in spite of all you could do to keep them steady.
There were, however, as I said before, wonderfully few
accidents; and I am happy to say that, in the many
hundreds of miles I have travelled by them and driven
them, I never saw a coach turned over.

THERE are a few small hints that may seem almost useless, and which many will say 'everybody knows,' but which, however, are not known by half those who have never driven 'down the Road,' and they will, I trust, excuse me for supposing that they do not know them. There are many little dodges which a gentleman with a well-broken, smart team in Hyde Park has never had, nor probably ever will have, a chance of knowing.

I will begin with saying, Never get into a mess if you can possibly keep out of one; but, if you do chance to get into a scrape, take care to get out of it well. 'Discretion is the better part of valour,' I have heard, and I believe it to be true; there is no great art required to get into a mess, but there is sometimes much difficulty in keeping out of one. I have more than once seen a fool-hardy fellow, under the influence of something stronger than toast-and-water, get into

'a scrawl' when he might have kept out of it, and
then, with all his dash and swagger, cut up as helpless and ignorant of how to get out of it as if he had
been 'a born fool,' which very probably was the case
with him.   A coach is a dangerous thing, if all don't
go right; and though I have seen many men do their
best to upset a coach without succeeding, still, when
least expected, it's as easily done as upsetting an old
woman's apple stall.

Should you come to grief with one of your horses,
should one fall down dead, or get the staggers, or
break one of his legs, or from some cause be so full
of pain that you can't get him on, and are obliged to
take him out of the coach, and drive home or to the
end of your stage or journey without him, of course
you must leave him on the road, and make an
'unicorn,' or what we used to call a 'pickaxe team.'
In case of accident, and for making the said 'pickaxe,'
particularly if going a long journey, it is a prudent
measure to carry a spare small bar, with the eye or
a ring set contrary way to the usual eye on a small
bar.   The ordinary eye will not let your small bar
sit the right way on your pole-hook.   As a set of

spare bars are generally carried behind a drag, a bar of the description I name may as well be carried instead of one of the ordinary small bars. You never require more than one of either kind, and the bar I have named is the only useful one in case of the sort of accident I have mentioned. The natural thing to do would be to put your main bar on; you would, however, find that, from the span being so much wider in the main bar than in the ordinary bar, your traces would not be long enough, and in all probability, if you did get them on, when your leader was in and pulling hard up-hill, the hooks of your main bar would be pulled into all kinds of shapes, and perhaps broken off altogether. This I have seen happen, and though, luckily, one is not often called upon to drive a ' pickaxe,' the wrinkle is worth knowing before such a mishap takes place. In coaching days of old, a bar such as I have described was generally to be found, amongst other ' arcana,' in the hind boot.

Always carry a spare trace, or, what is better, a chain trace. It takes but little room in one of your boots, and has more than once stood my friend. It is seldom wanted, it is true, but it is there if it should be wanted, and you may sometimes find it a handy thing for other purposes if you are away from home. I have seen a trace go when least expected, and in such a case, if you have not a spare trace of some kind, you're 'in a fix,' and if at night in a 'regular fix.' Therefore, always have a chain trace in your boot, about a foot and a half longer than your ordinary leather trace, with a ring at one end big enough for your chain to drop through, to make a loop to go over your roller-bolt, and a hook at the other end that will go into the links of your chain, that you may take your trace up or let it out as you would do with a leather trace and a buckle. On a gentleman's coach the breaking of a trace is of very rare occurrence, and in Hyde Park, or anywhere near town, a spare trace could be borrowed at almost any moment; but in the country, and if you go any distance or any excursion, something of the kind in case of accident is a 'sine quâ non,' and therefore commend me to a 'chain trace,' or you may be left on the road looking as helpless as a pump without a handle.

Don't think me an old muff, if I say don't drive
in London and round the Park, where you no doubt
wish to look smart, without bearing reins. I don't
mean to say, bear your horses up as if their heads
and tails were tied together, but use bearing reins.
Your team will look smarter, and you will have more
comfort with them than without them. It is very
seldom that four horses all carry their heads in the
right place, and if one or two of them are inclined to
get their heads down, it not only looks bad, but it is
a considerable nuisance to the driver to have to carry
his horses' heads, to prevent them lolling them
against the pole-hook, and perhaps catching their
bits in the pole-chains, which I have seen occur more
than once. In former days I remember bearing reins
on 'the Road.' They were discarded, from the fancy,
I suppose, that horses worked freer without them.
I think they did; but if they got a bit tired, or if
they were not of a good sort, they often got their
heads down and lolled about, and bored till they
made your arms ache.

The principal thing in old coaching days, however,
was to get them along and keep your time, and so

long as they did it, it did not much signify whether
they carried their heads quite in the right place or
not. A great point was to be able to use your whip
pretty well, and to be able to 'lift a horse up and
set him down again half a mile on the road,' and
unless you could do this on some roads it did not
signify much about bearing reins or no bearing reins.
During the latter part of my coaching I never saw
either a bearing rein or a buckle to a rein. Formerly,
all reins were buckled. I remember, when a little
chap going to school, it was a high honour to be on
the box, and to be allowed to unbuckle the reins as
you came to the change. Gradually, it became the
fashion not to buckle the reins, but to let them
hang down unbuckled ; and then it became the fashion
to have no buckles at all on the reins, and for twenty
years, and on fast coaches particularly, I never saw
such a thing as a buckle. It's a safe plan, nevertheless, to buckle your reins ; and with the thin, dandy,
new, slippery reins of the present day, it is positively
necessary to have them buckled, or they will very
easily slip through your fingers. With smart gloves
and thin reins, and very often new ones, if a man

has a single horse that pulls a little, his reins must
keep slipping through his fingers, and he must keep
pulling at his reins as if he was playing the harp,
which is inadmissible.   Have your reins long enough,
have them strong enough, say full an eighth of an
inch thick, have them broad enough, not less than a
full inch in width, they will then be stiff enough for
you to slip them up between your fingers, instead of
pulling at them from behind your hand, like Barber
pulling the strings of a pigeon trap at a match.   In
wet weather what a horrible thing are wet reins ;
positively they get like a 'yard of tripe.'   If thin,
they get limp very soon ; even if thick they will get
wet through in time.   If your gloves get wet through,
too, which they must do, your reins slip through
your fingers and you feel miserably helpless, and as
if you were driving with reins made of soap.   How
I have yearned, when in such a fix, for the old, thick,
well-greased reins of the old mail and the old coach
of former days.   You could hold your horses with
such reins, and though they did smell strongly of
neatsfoot oil and train oil, and other abominations
only known to the horsekeepers, on a wet day they

were a really great comfort, even if you had not a
pair of worsted gloves to put on in case of rain.
These never omit to take with you, as on a rainy
day they are the only thing through which the reins
don't slip, and they are on such an occasion a '*sine
quâ non.*' Always have them about your coach. You
may often want them when you least expect it. It
is not necessary for a man to walk about with an
umbrella on a fine day. But I say, when it's fine,
take your umbrella; when it rains, do as you like
about it.

Horses don't require a whip in these days, but no
one can drive without a whip, any more than Paganini
could play the fiddle without his fiddlestick. It is
now seldom required, but when required there are
very few that can use it. They ought to be able to
use the whip if necessary, but it is lamentable sometimes to see what an incumbrance the whip seems to
be, and how awkwardly it is handled.

It is laughable to see the length of whip sometimes adopted. This at once denotes a ' muff.' There
is no use in having a whip as tall as the monument,
with a thong as long as Piccadilly; a foot and a half

of thong and point together, hanging below your hand, gets entangled with your reins and anything else it comes in contact with. Some may say, ' I can't reach my leaders if it's shorter.' This is not a fact; you can if you do it 'according to Cocker,' and are not what is called a 'regular gardener.' The correct length for a whip, according to William and Joseph Ward of Newington, who are all dead and gone, was 5 ft. 1½in. from the end of the butt to the holder, and for the thong 12 ft. 5 or 6 in. from the holder to the end of the point ; anything more is superfluous. Rest to their souls ; they are all gone, I trust, with the good niggers. They were the best whipmakers in the world, as was proved by ninety out of a hundred coachmen using their whips on every road in the kingdom. Almost any saddler, however small, in towns where a coach passed through, had them, and I have seen them produced in bundles to choose from. They were not only first-rate, but very cheap, com- pared with the price one pays in these days ; twelve or fourteen shillings would produce quite a swell whip, and I have bought really good ones, with plain leather handles, three for a guinea. These were without ferrules of any kind, and, if the stick turned out good, were ferruled afterwards. A whip of the same kind, with brass ferrules used to cost ten shillings ; one with silver ferrules was hardly known, except on the Lord Mayor's coach, or to drive the judge at the assizes. I remember giving a swell coachman a swell whip, which cost me half my pocket-money when a youngster, and instead of being very grateful for the little attention, he turned up his nose at it and said, 'Why did you give me such a thing as this ? Why did you not give me one of Ward's ?' Of course I pocketed the compliment and wished I had, as I should have saved ten or twelve shillings. I never liked the fellow afterwards, and as he had taught me something I profited by his lesson, but I never gave him any more whips. His name was Sam Spiller ; he drove the 'Regent' coach from Huntingdon to London, down Mondays, Wednesdays, and Fridays ; up Tuesdays, Thursdays, and Saturdays. Whilst on the subject of whips, let me say a word to those who are ambitious to learn that gentle art. There appeared in 'Land and Water,' some little time since, the following :—

'Sir :

'My son is perfectly crazy about driving four-in-hand. Hang the expense, he says, &c., &c.'

His governor seems full of money, for he goes on to say : 'That I don't mind.' Something like a governor! But whatever you or your governor may do, do not pretend to drive till you can catch your whip properly. Nothing looks so cocktail and muffish on a coach as to see a man learning to catch his whip, and after many futile efforts taking it upside down for this purpose, and twisting the thong round and round with the point downwards, as if he was stirring porridge for a pack of hounds.

'But how is a fellow to learn to catch his whip?' you may say. To this, I reply, 'If you are such an awkward fellow as not to be able to learn to catch it, and almost by instinct, shut yourself up in your room, put a chair upon your table, harness four chairs together, get a stiff top joint of your fishing rod, if you have one, or any light stick that will do duty for one, plait some whipcord, and make a thong

twice as long as your stick, and having seated yourself upon your chair for a box, learn to catch your
whip there, and in private, and learn to hit your
horses all round; they cannot run away or upset your
coach, if you are careful. Catch up your thong, and
hit your wheelers, then untwist it and hit your leaders
first on the off-side, it is the easiest to begin with,
then on the near side, then first one and then the
other, one, two, three, and a draw, and so on the
other side. You may in these days never be called
upon to hit a horse at all, but you ought to be able
to do it, and if you can't do it you are not a coachman, though you may fancy you are, and may get on
pretty well with a flash team in Hyde Park, where
you have nothing to do but hold your reins and
steer clear of your friends and neighbours.

Never divide your reins, if you can possibly avoid
it, or you will have to 'club-haul' them, which is inadmissible. If you divide your reins you will have to
get another hand to hold your whip, and another, if you
chance to have to go down a pitch, to put on your
patent break. The handle of this instrument must
be much in your way. It makes your coach look very

ugly, and should be behind, under the control of him
who acts as guard or ' shooter.' I don't believe that one
man in a thousand knows what a ' shooter' means ; and
if he ever heard of such an important personage, I
will venture to say he cannot say from whence the
term is derived. I have often heard a man say, ' Oh !
I'll be shooter,' which meant to say, I will act as guard,
and put on and take off the skid at the bottom of the
hills and steep pitches, or, as we used to call them, ' a
steep shoot.' This many, no doubt, thought gave the
name of ' shooter' to the guard ; this, however, was not
the real ' unde derivatur.' The real derivation was
from ' Shooter's Hill,' on the London and Dover Road,
which all heavy coaches, and indeed the mails,[1] used
to ' skid ' down, and from taking off the skid at the
bottom of ' Shooter's Hill,' the guard on a coach used
to get the name of the ' shooter.' On a fast coach this
was a responsible office, and an office that demanded a
great deal of quickness and knack. I have often seen
the skid put on without stopping the coach, the pace

---

[1] I have heard the name of the ' shooter' accounted for, because
on a mail the guard carried a blunderbuss and pistols to shoot Dick
Turpin and such fellows with, but I believe the other reason is the
right one.

only stayed a little, and the skid slung, as it were, into
its place under the wheel, with a ' right.' It is a dangerous thing to trust too much to your skid, for if anything happens to go, you are worse off than if you had
none at all. I, however, remember once nearly coming
to grief from not having a skid on. We were going
into Henley, and in going down Henley Hill, when
more than half down, the horses holding the coach
without any skid on, the near wheeler's pole chain by
some means came undone. I was a stranger on that
road, and was sitting by the side of the coachman, whose
name I forget, or perhaps never knew. A passenger,
evidently a Methodist parson, or a lugubrious-looking
fellow of some kind, with a white choker and a face
as long as a two-foot rule, would from time to time
' discourse' the coachman, and give him a tract, or
something of the kind. This he at once stuffed into his
pocket, with a ' Thank you, sir; I have no time for
reading.' No doubt the man was a worthy man in his
place; but out of his place on a coach with one of the
pole-chains gone. Of course, as soon as the chain
came undone there was nothing for it but to look out
for a piece of gravel to run the wheel on, and keep the

wheelers away from the splinter-bar. There was, however, no gravel, no loose stones, or any assistance of
that kind ; and my friend the coachman had his hands
full to keep the coach from running over his wheelers.
A patent drag would have come in well under such circumstances, but in those days they were not invented.
In the midst of this little dilemma what should my
friend with the long face and white choker do but
offer him another tract. Jehu, however, was intent
upon his business, and muttered in not a very pleasant
tone, ‘ Oh dear ! oh dear ! whatever can I do with
your papers ; how ever can you be a giving me papers
now ; no skid on, pole-chain gone, and never a bit of
gravel as I can see to run a wheel on. I don't see
as we shan't be over yet ; so if you happens to know
anything short, sir, now's your time.’ I was sitting
beside the coachman, and really at one time began to
fear that we should not get safely to the bottom of the
hill. He knew his business well, however, and from
the fact of having started quietly off the crown of the
hill, being very cool and collected, and having a very
slight load, only the man in black and me, we did not
come to grief. There's nothing like a bit of loose

gravel to run your wheel up'n, and many is the time
I have looked out for some loose gravel or fresh
broken stones; they are a wonderful help in times of
need.   Recollect that if your pole-chains go or get
loose going down a hill, and no skid on, it's a somewhat serious business.   Your 'valour' will be of use,
because it will help you to keep your head cool; but
your 'discretion' will be found your best friend.   As
you will have no 'steerage way,' you will have to do
the thing 'gingerly,' to keep your coach from running
on to your wheeler or over him, and setting him kicking, and perhaps finding him altogether in the front
boot, or perhaps inside the coach with your lady passengers.   On such an occasion look out for the bit of
gravel, which is the only thing that can save you from
becoming 'mixed biscuits' before you get to the bottom
of the hill.

'Patent drags' have so taken the place of the old
'skid' that my old friend the 'shooter' is seldom seen
or heard of now. I have in former days seen an amateur
'shooter' come to sad grief, and like others who try a
game they don't understand, 'burn their fingers.' I
remember many years ago, that an old friend and schoolfellow of mine, and of the other two 'little boys in their
long drab great coats,' were on the old ' Regent ' coach,
on their way back to Eton. My old school-fellow, who
is now a dignitary of the Church, and lives close to his
brother's place, Connington Castle, in Huntingdonshire,
would aspire to the dignified post of ' shooter.' The
old Stamford ' Regent ' did not carry a guard of any
kind. Our amateur guard put the 'skid' on in a most
workmanlike manner at the top of a hill, whose name I
at this moment forget, but it was not far from Stilton,
of *cheese* fame—and jumped down to perform the *opposite*
feat at the *bottom* of the hill. ' Mind what you're at,

old friend ' (for that was a favourite term of endearment
of ' Old John's '). said Old John Barker, as he looked
behind the coach : ' you'll burn your fingers if you don't
mind.'   But, alas! he was *too late*; the young ' guard '
had seized the ' skid,' which was ' as hot as pepper,'
almost red hot, fast by the neck, and with a shriek of
agony ' dropped it like a hot potato.'   Poor George
Heathcote, for he it was, is alive still, and I feel sure
cannot have forgotten the circumstance.   The pain he
suffered all the way to London was intense, with all the
skin of his right hand scorched and blistered in a
terrible way.   I can see him even now, in my mind's
eye, carrying his unfortunate blistered fingers in a large
teacup of brandy which we procured at the first ' dealer
in spiritous liquors ' that we came across on the way.
He did not act amateur ' shooter ' any more *that* journey,
and though I used to travel with him on various occasions afterwards, I don't remember that he ever again
patronized the same trade, and I believe to this day he
fancies that everything in the shape of *iron must be hot.*

As we are on the subject of fire, and my old friend with his burnt fingers, in which ' Old John Barker ' and the Regent coach are again mentioned, an anecdote of how ' Old John ' and a certain ' Bill Jenkins ' got a refractory team to start, may amuse. On one memorable occasion he could not get his team to start; nothing could make them; no *persuasion* could prevail. At last ' Old John ' said, ' Bill, get us a couple of wisps of straw and a lantern.' ' Bill,' in obedience to his orders, set some straw on fire under the refractory horses, the effect was *electrical*, and away they went at once, ' as if the devil had kicked them endways.'

This is something like the story of a gentleman in Ireland. The mare he was riding hated the sight of a blacksmith's shop, and on his coming up to one on the road, no earthly power would get her to pass it. The good-hearted blacksmith, like a true Irishman, wished to tender his assistance, and going into his smithy brought out a red-hot horseshoe in his tongs or pincers, saying ' Lang life to your Hanour. The devil a bit will *she* pass it ; *will* I clap a warm iron to the mare yer Hanour ? '

If you drive out of your own stable-yard, or indeed out of any yard, and particularly at night, if you drive home from Greenwich, feeling ' pretty full of fish,' always go round your horses, and see that all your reins are buckled, and that your coupling reins are crossed.

I do not doubt that your coachman or groom is a steady fellow, but at times he will eat a good deal of fish as well as his master; and if he does this, such little accidents may happen. As four eyes are better than two, it is always a safe precaution to go round your horses and see that all is right, your reins buckled, and so forth, before you get on the box.

Having been caught myself once, I have no hesitation in giving this little bit of advice. I was driving on the road between Chester and Bangor, and on going round my horses at Abergele I found that my leaders' coupling reins were not crossed, and that the fool of a horsekeeper had buckled both reins to the same horse ; what might have happened had we started I do not know.   As it was, I saw it in time ; and on my remarking, ' Why, Jack,' or Bill, or whatever his name was, ' you don't expect I'm going to start in this form ? ' he said, ' Well, inteed, it's forgotten to cross the reins, however, this time.'

SHOULD you be driving on a road, such as from London to Epsom or Ascot, on one of the race days, when all is stir and confusion, and everything and everybody rushing for the toll-bar, and everyone in ' whisky, buggy, dog-cart, gig, chaise, curricle, or tandem,' is trying who can get through first without paying ; on such an occasion keep your eyes open, or perhaps, just as you get to the gate, the toll-bar keeper will shut it in your leaders' faces. Then you will either be through the gate or have to pull them all up of a heap, neither of which is quite pleasant ; but on such an occasion one of these feats must be performed ' experto crede.' It is now some years since, when returning from Ascot, and on a piping hot day, I well remember, on arriving within six or seven miles of London, with hundreds of vehicles of all kinds making the best of their way to get through the toll-bar ; and though my servant held

his ticket out so that the toll-bar keeper could not
help seeing it, I felt a sort of presentiment that the
scoundrel looked as if he meant to shut the gate upon
me. With this little warning, I caught my horses up
pretty short, and was ready for anything that might
happen. My suspicions were correct, for as I came
within ten yards of the gate the vagabond stepped
across the road and slammed the gate in my leaders'
faces. He then as quickly, seeing that he was in the
wrong, pulled the gate open again, and stood looking
at me. My whip happened to be caught up in the
most approved style. I made a feint at him by just
cocking up my elbow; he made a duck and put up
his arm, thinking I was going to hit him, which was
the real state of the case. The day being piping hot,
he was in his shirt sleeves. As he ducked, I saw
well under his arm, and I gave him such a soaker in
the ribs that he fairly squealed again. One of my passengers declared I had broken one of his ribs, and that
he heard it go ; but as I never heard of his being taken
to St. George's Hospital, I hope it was not the case.
Perhaps I was wrong in hitting him; but I could not
help it; the provocation was too great. My whip was

caught up so beautifully, and his ribs, when he lifted his elbow and ducked, looked so tempting, that if I had known I was to be hanged for it, I don't think I could have thrown away the chance of giving him that one ' soaker.'

AN OLD COACHMAN.

READER, should you chance to be an old coachman, one of the olden time, who has seen coaching as it once was, you will know many of the scenes I have attempted to describe; you will be able to call to mind, I may say, the look of the whole affair itself. You will be able to recall the coachmen and guards, and the very horses you have driven; the foggy mornings out of London; the 'Peacock' at Islington; the pretty barmaid who used to give you your glass of rum-and-milk; the cold, snowy days and nights that you have passed on the mail or coach; the guard and his yard of tin, on the mail, wakening up the drowsy toll-bar keeper at unheard-of hours at night and early morning. You will remember the cheery keyed bugle of the guard on the coach, upon which he played, 'Oh, dear, what can the matter be?' or some such lively tune, as he passed through the different towns in the middle of the night, much to the disturbance of some of the quietly snoozing population, it is to be feared. You will recollect

many a tedious day and night, with snow on the
ground and snow falling all around, when you were
obliged to have a pair of leaders to help to pull you
through the snow and up the hills, and how, when
frosty and slippery, you had to screw your horses from
one side of the road to the other to get them up the
hill at all. You will have a lively recollection of the
bitter cold that pervaded your half-frozen form, and
the dire hunger that had taken possession of your
inner man, and how it was almost impossible to un-
button your great-coat, and get off your ample neck-
handkerchief, which was often wet through, before you
could eat your dinner, which was announced by the
coachman as, 'Now, gentlemen, twenty minutes for
dinner!' These twenty minutes in reality seemed but
five. By the time you had got your hands a little
warm and your mouth into eating trim, he would put
his head in again and inform you most politely : 'Now,
gentlemen, please, the coach is ready ;' and thus between getting your wet coats, &c., off, and putting
your wet coats, &c., on, there was but little eating to
be done in the twenty minutes. To the tune of two-
and-sixpence a head, and sixpence for the waiter.

You will, no doubt, remember the look of the streets as you entered London about six o'clock of a winter's morning; how dimly the oil-lamps used to burn at that time of day, and how seedy the old 'Charlie' used to look, and how red his old nose used to be with the cold, and the 'goes down of gin' he had had during 'the night. You will remember the smell of the steam from the horses, as you passed under the arch of the 'Swan and Two Necks,' Lad Lane, or into the yard of the 'Bull and Mouth.' You will remember the look of utter desolation that reigned around as you entered the inns at six o'clock in the morning in winter. All were inns in those days; there were no hotels : and the 'nothing to be had to eat' feeling that came over your hungry stomach when the dirty half-starved housemaid told you that nobody except the bookkeeper was up yet. You will remember all these little circumstances, and many more that I could name. You would remember, no doubt, that a guard's horn on a mail used actually to be made of tin ; and from their being nearly a yard, or in reality about two feet, of that precious metal, it got the name of the 'yard of tin.' You may also remember that in

olden times it went into a sort of holder, almost like
a lamp-iron, on the off-side of the body of the mail,
and in later days into a kind of leather socket; and
that the brass horn, in its long wicker basket, was an
innovation upon that melodious musical instrument
called the 'grunting stick,' or 'yard of tin,' of former
days. You will remember, no doubt, that on a stage
coach a long horn was seldom or ever carried—indeed,
I may say never; but that it was always a keyed bugle,
slung in a basket on the off-side the back seat, and that
there was generally a thick piece of netting stretched
across the off-side of the seats behind the coach, to
prevent umbrellas, coats, and various things, including
old women, from tumbling overboard. The guard on
a coach used always to get up and down, as did the
passengers, on the near side. In these days one sees
the long horn basket, if one is carried at all, anywhere
and everywhere but in the right place, and if anyone
tries to blow the horn anything but the right music
comes out of it. I saw a coach coming down Piccadilly some little time since; a fellow in a red hunting-
coat was performing on a long horn, and trying to get
out a note that was not on the instrument. There

are only two notes, or should not be more; and as
he was using a great deal of exertion to get out three,
I was in hopes the horn would burst and blow his
brains out : and I watched the coach for some distance
with the hope of seeing this occur, but was disappointed.

You will remember, if you have ever travelled by
the 'Stamford Regent,' and have had Tom Hennesy
for coachman, how his shrill whistle, which was nearly
as loud as that on the present railway, but more melodious, would waken up the horses, and make them
skip up into their collars, for fear that he was going
to administer it to them all round. You will remember
all these little incidents, and many more.

You will say and think with me, I dare say, that
in spite of wet and cold, frost and snow, and all the
variations of temperature that one used to go through
on a coach, both by day and night, they were jolly
times, 'awfully jolly,' as they say in these fast days.
You will, as I do, look back upon those days with
pleasure, and

> ' Though the coachmen of old are dead,
>   Though the guards are turned to clay,
>   You will still remember the " yard of tin,"
>   And the mail of the olden day.'

You will look with pleasure upon the rising generation as they come into the Park with their smart
coaches and teams, and you will admire them for
being 'chips of the old block,' and being fond of
coaching ; and though they may not all seem to know
their business quite as well as those who have really
'been on the Road,' you will make every allowance
for what you see amiss, and bestow your praises
upon the many that really deserve it ; for many there
are who, though they have had no chance of regular
road work, look like workmen and handle their horses
well. I had the pleasure of seeing the first start
of the new blue coats and yellow buttons from the
Marble Arch, some time since. I think there were
about twenty-four coaches. I fully expected to see
a great many muffs, and a great many collisions, and
some real good accidents. This, however, was not the
case. I saw no collision, and I saw no accident.
The space that was supposed to be kept for the
coaches was not kept at all. There were carriages
and every kind of vehicle all over the place, and the
whole arrangements were disgraceful. Yet I saw
none of the blue coats get into grief. They came up

to take the places which ought to have been kept
clear for them, if not by the police, by the courtesy
of those looking on, without any great difficulty, and
they threaded through the numerous vehicles like
workmen. I own I was most agreeably disappointed
and surprised to see so creditable a performance, and
I felt inclined more than once to take my hat off to
them. To say that I did not see 'a muff' at all
would not be true; I did see one or two, and one in
particular, who, if he has not learnt his trade better
since the day I speak of, will have to listen to the
customary compliment, 'Better stay at home,' or, for
his own safety and that of the public, 'bring his
nurse with him.' To him, whoever he may be, and
to any other that may be like him, I give this parting
advice :—

Do not divide your reins, and sit with them in
two hands nearly up to your chin, with your friend
holding your whip. Do not carry a long-horn in a
wicker basket by the side of the handle of your
patent break ; it looks very unworkmanlike. I am sure
you cannot find hands or time to use it, and added to
this, it is quite the wrong place for a horn, which on
a gentleman's drag is rather out of place at any time.

If you must carry a horn, let it be behind, on the
off-side of your coach. No coachman can find time
to 'sound his own trumpet.' His hands are required
for better purposes. The bare idea of driving and
trumpeting at the same time is enough to call up
the spirits of defunct coachmen and guards. Always
have an apron on your box; it hides a bad seat and
a pair of bent knees better than anything, and you
look altogether more coaching with than without one.
Added to this, should you carry a 'petticoat on the
box,' it is convenient to hide those pretty little feet and
ankles which are so much admired in a ball-room, but
which should not appear on the outside of a coach.
Sit straight on your box, with your elbows close to
your side, your hands well down, your shoulders well
back, your head erect, and your eyes well in front of
you. Do not set your back up like a 'pig in a rage,
and don't bend over your footboard as if you were
looking after the stump of the cigar you have just
dropped. Above all things, do not sit with your knees
bent; sit with them straight, and not curled up to your
chin, and as if you were under the influence of a brisk
cathartic.

It's hard to say 'farewell,' it's anguish to murmur 'adieu;' but, as there must be an end to all things, so must I begin to wind up, and come to an end of what I dare hardly flatter myself has been of much interest to you to read. You have, however, kind reader, been most indulgent to have got thus far without pitching my 'little work' out of window, which perhaps you *would* have done, had it not in some measure beguiled your idle time. It would give me real pleasure to think that it *had* helped you to smoke your pipe more comfortably than you would have done had you had nothing else to occupy you but your own thoughts.

You will, I dare say, have thought many of the anecdotes stupid and uninteresting, and not very full of information, and that things that happened to me many years since do not keep pace with the times we now live in; and, above all, that I have bored you by talking too much of myself. This is all true; but as

the little book has been a book of my own doings,
reminiscences of the roads on which I loved to travel,
and facts which have come within my own notice, you
must forgive 'a worn-out coachman' for talking too
much of himself, and clinging to old associations,
sayings, and doings, coachmen and guards, coaches
and horses, which have disappeared from the scene
for ever. Yes, reader, I am 'a worn-out coachman,'
going down-hill fast; too fast almost to be able
to think of the pace. 'Then why don't you put on
your break?' I think I hear you say. But to this I
reply : 'It's of no use ; we're close to the bottom of
the hill, and when we get there we shall stóp, whether
we like it or no.' During the many years I drove
I always found that I had something to learn, and
the more I drove, the more I seemed to learn something. Every journey and every stage I went I was
sure to get a wrinkle of some kind.

Though I am well aware that some who may
read this may have picked up more wrinkles than
I have, I feel quite sure that there are many who
have not. In my early days I never was too proud
to learn anything ; I could splice a thong or put on

a point with any man, and I used to fancy I could
work a coach as well as most ' gentlemen coachmen.'
All these, then useful accomplishments, are now of
little or no use. The rail and 'Anno Domini' have
got the better of us all. Mails, coaches, coachmen,
guards, horns, horses, horsekeepers, and even the toll-
bar gates are gone, and few, very few, alas! of us
remain. ' *Pristinæ virtutis memores.*'

ALAS! ALAS! WHERE IS IT GONE?

Alas ! alas ! where is it gone,
    That coach with its four bright bays?
Alas ! alas ! where is it gone,
    That spicy team of greys ?

Where is the coach ? where is the mail ?
    The coachman, where is he?
Where is the guard that used to blow
    His horn so cheerily?

Where is the guard that used to wake
    The still of the early morn,
And rouse the sleepy toll-bar man
    With the sound of the ' old mail horn '?

Alas ! alas ! where are they gone,
    The coach and the bays and greys?
Alas ! alas ! where is it gone,.
    That ' light of other days '?

The sun has set that once shone out
    So bright upon those teams ;
The night has come, and all that's past
    Seems but as fleeting dreams.

No more the sleepy toll-bar man
    Is roused at early morn,
And turns reluctant out of bed
    With a curse on that long tin horn.

No more in his nightshirt, as of old,
　And his nightcap on his pate,
Does he hurry across the frozen road
　To open the turnpike gate.

No more as he's just turned into bed,
　And has just got warm again,
Is he doomed to attend to his toll-bar gate,
　And battle with snow and rain.

He snoozes all night till broad daylight ;
　His slumbers at early dawn
Are not disturbed by the old mail coach,
　Nor the sound of the old mail horn.

The mail, the horn, the coachman, guard,
　Are nowhere to be found ;
The four bright bays that used to trot
　With that ' quadrupedante' sound

Are dead and gone, the gate is gone;
　All now is still around ;
For the coachman and guard and the four bright bays
　Lie four foot under the ground.

Alas ! for the days that are past and gone,
　For those palmy days of old.
Alas ! for the joyous hearts that then
　Beat warm, but now are cold ;

Are cold and silent in the grave,
　With all their jovial sounds :
The coachman and guards and their teams are gone
　To the happy hunting grounds.

WHILST my 'Reminiscences of a Gentleman Coachman' are in the press, one or two kind friends who
are much interested in all proceedings connected with
the Road, have suggested to me that ' Down the Road'
will hardly be perfect without some notice being taken
of Modern Coaching. Indeed, I am told in the following words, 'That the book would be most incomplete
without the "modern turn-out;" that a few remarks
on the present Coaching Clubs, and of their principal
members; in fact, a few lines of what is going on in
the present day, would be a great addition.'

I sincerely thank those kind friends for their good
opinion of my power to describe what I know but
little about. I am what is called ' out of the betting '
in these fast days; and I must leave it to some
younger hand and abler pen to speak of the year
1874, its smart coaches, and gaudy high-stepping two-
hundred-guinea horses, with those ' chips of the old

block' behind them, who in so praiseworthy a way aspire to the rekindling of the 'light of other days.'

My lot was not cast in the days of smart coaches, and gaudy high-stepping two hundred guinea horses, and I must be content with my 'Reminiscences' of the past.

It is seldom that I am to be seen in 'Babylon' now-a days; that famed city has few charms for me; but when I *do* go there, I find myself occasionally in Piccadilly, and gazing at the coaches; and, as the spider said to the fly, 'You'll see so many curious things you never saw before,' so do *I*. I see coaches without any luggage on them. Coachmen with their reins in two hands, a kind of erection on the top of the coach, like in shape to what a pot-boy in olden times used to carry pewter-pots full of beer in, but on a much larger scale. This, I am informed, is called a 'knifeboad;' and upon this passengers desirous of seeing the country, from what I consider a danger-ous elevation, are sitting, not like the sparrow of old, 'alone,' but in a row. This, I have been told, is an improvement; but in my humble, and perhaps ignorant and superannuated opinion, I do not seem to see it.

Added to this, I have seen a coachman pull up his horses at the far-famed ' White Horse Cellar ' with his reins in two hands, and then put on his ' patent break,' I suppose, to stop his coach, lest his horses should move on, which, in olden days they were not much inclined to do, after they had done their ten miles an hour, with ' twelve out and four in,' and luggage in proportion.

Such curious things have appeared to my astonished vision ; but I am constrained to suppose that I am ' an old-fashioned Fogy,' and that it must be all right ; and that, as I was informed at ' Hatchett's,' on a certain day, by a certain somebody connected with the afore-said ' knifeboard,' that there were many improvements on the old ' stage-coach.' ' Query ?' thinks I to myself.

Times are so changed since I cut my first teeth, and even since I cut my wise teeth (if you can imagine, good reader, that I ever cut them at all), that a thorough coaching-looking ' Jehu ' is not to be seen. The sons and grandsons of the old-fashioned ' Down the Road,' with the present fashion of beards and moustaches, cannot, do what they will, look like the

coachman of the olden day, who was ' sui generis '
as to look, thought, and deed.   He looked differently
altogether, he thought differently altogether ; and if
by chance you saw him off his ' rostrum,' he walked,
carried his whip, and had a different air about him,
and a different cut altogether.   He seemed to have
written on his back, as he passed you, ' I am So-
and-so,' and drive the ' Defiance,' ' Tally-ho,' ' Regulator,'
' The Wonder,' ' The Hirondelle,' or some such noted
coach.   No ! good reader.   The race is all but extinct,
and I know of no mixture of breed that would
produce the like again.

Alas ! how *can* it be otherwise, now that all the
great roads of former days are overgrown with
weeds, the coaches broken up, or perhaps turned
into hen-roosts, and the tea-kettle with its unmelo-
dious whistle has taken such full possession of every
thing and everybody and everybody's luggage.   I do
not know of more than two or three men now
living whom I have ever seen on a coach — a real
stage-coach.   There may be some others ; but, as they
did not frequent the same road as your humble servant,
I cannot speak of their merits, except from hearsay.

I was 'wending my weary way' down that once much patronised lounge, Bond Street, one hot summer's afternoon, whence those who 'took their post-time therein,' in days of yore, got the name of ' Bond Street Swells.' It was about 5 P.M., as they now have it, and the gaudy Dowagers, in their gaudy equipages, were passing and repassing, and like a swarm of ants were taking the air, or enjoying the sun, which was fairly 'piping,' and I thought almost capable of roasting me alive. When at the corner of Bond Street and Piccadilly, close to a well-known biscuit-shop, and opposite Christie's, the noted hatter, I recognised a back I thought I ought to know; and on my laying my hand upon his shoulder, my old acquaintance turned round. 'I suppose you want to cross,' said I. 'You'll stand a chance of getting run over if you do'—for there was a great crush of carriages. 'I don't want to cross,' said he. ' I'm only waiting to see some of these fellows run against each other! I can't make it out! How the devil do they manage to get round the corner in such a crowd, without coming to grief, driving, as they do, with their reins in both hands?'

G G

Sir Richard Bulkley—for he it was—could 'do the trick' well himself, and was as pretty a coachman as need be, and could 'fan 'em along' as well as here and there one. No wonder that he should be interested in seeing such an edifying performance, which we both agreed was marvellous. Another old coaching friend, who has seen 'the light of other days,' and is still holding his own with the present generation, encouraging the 'gentle art' by every means in his power, must not be forgotten. Those who live in the neighbourhood of Wrexham and Chester will hardly have forgotten the cheery, good-looking young guardsman who used at times to drive the 'Oak' and 'Nettle' coaches between the aforesaid towns. 'Captain Stracey,' or 'Tom Stracey,' as he was then called (though his real name was 'Edward'), was a real lover of 'the Road.' It was a pleasant sight to see him, looking all over the workman he was, and still is. Though since those days he has changed his name to that of Colonel Stracey Clitherow, and like myself has become longer in the tooth than he was twenty years ago, like the old huntsman he loves to hear the crack of the whip and the sound of the horn, and is to be found horsing and driving one of the coaches out of London, which, if he has not forgotten the olden days, he can do as well as anyone.

Dear old pal! if any 'vet.' were to look into our mouths he would find, I am afraid, that *you* have a considerable advantage over me in that respect. We have, however, been friends together in 'sunshine and in shower;' and though parted as regards coaching in these days, you will probably smile when you read this, and say, 'Why, Charlie, you surely have never been such an old fool at your time of life as to get into print! You'll either get off the road or upset the coach altogether.'

It seems but the other day, though 'tis twenty years ago at least, that when I pulled up at the 'Feathers' office at Chester, and inquired of the book-keeper, a certain Mr. Nutt, whether he had seen Captain Stracey lately, 'No, sir,' he replied, 'I have not : I wish I *did* see him oftener, bless him ; I *do* like to see him, he always brings his horses up " so nice," and he *do* always look *so* pleasant ! '

How many old friends of former coaching days are gone from amongst us since the times I have been

speaking of, and how few remain to tell the tale of
former glory, I dare not think. I could mention some
few who I am aware *have* been 'down the Road,' but
never having driven in their company, I am not able
to speak of their merits, except by repute.

Of those who *are* gone from amongst us, I *will* not
speak. 'De mortuis nil nisi bonum, requiescant in pace.'

Of the rising generation I am not competent to
speak ; I have not the pleasure of knowing many of
them ; and though I admire their love of 'the Road,' and
their smart coaches and smart teams, it would, I feel, be
highly unbecoming in me to attempt (as I have been
requested to do) to give any opinion of the merits
of the 'modern turn-out.' I should get into such hot
water as would be past bearing. It has been, no
doubt, with a kind intention that I have been asked
to insert a chapter or two upon 'Coaching and Coaches
of the Present Day ;' and I am grateful for the compliment paid me by those who suppose I could do so.
I cannot, however, presume to criticise, and must leave
it to some one who is more conversant with the doings
of Anno Domini 1874. If I had the will or the power
of describing one turn-out as better than another, in

these days when everyone is trying to be first, and vieing who can have the *best* and most *expensive* team and so forth, jealousy would put in its hateful nose at once—for it must be well known to all men 'how happy we mortals might be if jealousy did not exist' —and that whatever is done by the B's the C's try to do more than equal, whether they have the same means or not. Hence, if any presumptuous writer were to have the audacity to hint that B's leaders were too far from the wheelers, or that C's pole was too long, and that B's was 'about the thing,' would there not be a regular 'shine,' and would not jealousy wink her jaundiced eye at him?

Among the very few men remaining that have ever *been* on a coach, surely there must be some one who can 'hit them all round,' if necessary. There may be some who have never seen a real, thorough-bred coach, and yet who are good coachmen ; to them I commend the task. I fear that I myself may 'come under the lash,' and stand a good chance of being pulled to pieces for my humble endeavours to describe some of the incidents of coaching days, and deeds long past and gone.

If I have accomplished what I have attempted, it will be a great satisfaction to think that I have attained my end. My task has been to avoid giving any opinion, humble and worthless as it might be, as to *who* can 'waggon' and *who* can not; whose is the best team and whose is not. I have not presumed to criticise. In fact, my aim has been to 'sing a song of other days'—to amuse, and not to offend.

LONDON: PRINTED BY
SPOTTISWOODE AND CO., NEW-STREET SQUARE
AND PARLIAMENT STREET

www.ingramcontent.com/pod-product-compliance
Lightning Source LLC
Chambersburg PA
CBHW021043030726
47496CB00006B/1667